The New Republic of Texas

El Diablo

by

Vernon Gillen

All of Vernon's book are available at Amazon.com

ISBN - #

978-1694737922

From the Author

I have been asked many times why I have people cursing in my novels if I am a Christian. Although I am a Christian the whole world is not. People curse and use foul language every day. In my novels I try to make it as realistic as possible. This means that some of the characters in my novels will curse. Sorry but that is the real world. However; I still never write God's name in vein.

I have been told; "Well I will not buy your novels then." That's okay. I do not write my novels in a make-believe world that you might live in. My characters live in the real world. I am sorry that you are not buying my novels but I am selling plenty to those that live in the real world. Some people have their heads so high in the clouds that they are no Earthly good. My novels are for the rest of you.

As you ready my novels you will see me mention Liberal Communist. This is because all Liberals and Democrats are in fact Communist. Right now all of the Democrats running for the Oval Office against Trump's second term are Socialist. Socialism is nothing but a milder version of Communism. If you vote for a Communist then you area Communist.

All writers put how they feel about things in their novels. It is our way of venting off our anger about things. In my novels you can see how I feel about all kinds of things.

Now something to the young writer. If you like to write or tell stories then just do it. Write about things you know. I am kind of like Steven King. I write about things that I feared as a child but also many thing that I fear right now. I feared a rogue president (Liberal) turning dictator so I wrote four novels in the *Texas Under Siege* series. At one time I feared North Korea and China invading our country so I wrote the four novels in *The Mountain Ghost* series. I don't really fear zombies all that much but I do use zombies in three of my novels *Black Blood,* the *Deadwalkers* and the third novel in *Texas Under Siege* series.

Write about what you know, what you like and think about

all of the time. The hardest part about writing is starting a novel. Almost every time I write a novel I go back to re-write the first chapter to match it with the rest of the novel. As I write my ideas change. When I start a novel I never know how it will end or what I will be writing in it. I just start with an idea and start writing. Then I allow my imagination to take over.

I may start a novel and run out of ideas. No problem. I start another novel and when I finish it I go back to the other novel and work on it. I cannot tell you how many times I have set aside the novel *Fire Dancers* and gone back to it.

Well; this is me. I hope you enjoy my novels. At the end of all of my novels I give you my e-mail address. Let me know what you think.

Now you know a little about what makes the writer

Vernon Gillen.

Contents

Chapter 1

Mart

After sixteen years of Democrat presidents almost destroying this nation a Republican president was elected that promised to make the United States a powerful nation again. He had a wall built on the southern border with Mexico.

After being re-elected the Republican President and Vice-President were assassinated and the Democrat Speaker of the House became our new President. With the Liberal Democrats completely in charge our nation quickly slid down hill again.

Taxes quickly climbed forcing many businesses to move back over seas. Within a year unemployment rose to thirty three percent. Crime in the cities quadrupled.

The New Black Panther Party, Black Lives Matters group, MS-13 members, and Antifa combined forces and declare war on all police officers and other civil servants. Within the first year after this declaration over 2,300 police officers are murdered execution style in the United States.

Texas and California is being given back to Mexico by the Democrats in the House and Senate in order to keep what little peace there was with Mexico. This decision is cleared by the new Liberal President.

Many Texans have had enough of the Liberal Communist running and ruining their country and choose to fight back. A second civil war starts in the United States. This is the story of some of those Texans that called themselves; The Texicans.

The Democrats in Congress and the Senate voted to raise the taxes 27% over night on the American citizens which mainly hit the middle class. This money was used to push the liberal agendas such as reinstating partial birth abortion, Welfare for illegal aliens, and the removal of the southern wall on the Mexican border.

The previous Republican president had built the twenty foot tall wall along seventy percent of the Mexican border. The new Socialist president with the Democrat controlled House and Senate hired Mexican construction companies to bulldoze the walls down.

All firearms larger than .22 caliber were outlawed. American citizens that had firearms larger than .22 caliber had sixty days to turn in their firearms to their local police departments. Anyone caught with these firearms after the sixty days would be thrown into prison for life.

One day the president admitted that he was a Muslim and had the word "God" on all currency replaced with the word "Ala". American money now said; "In Ala We Trust."

The Holy Bible was one of the many books that were

outlawed. No one was allowed to own one. Many Christian churches were shut down across the United States and any that remained lost their tax exempt status. Muslim Mosque were popping up everyplace and they continued their tax exempt status.

Freedom was all but completely gone. All Christians, Republicans, and good citizens were considered bad people and talk of civil war was on the lips of everyone. A line was being drawn in the sand. On one side were the Republicans, Christians, gun owners that had not turned in heir firearms, Veterans, police, and a few other like minded people. On the other side of the line were the Liberals, Democrats, Communist, Muslims, gang members and other criminals.

Finally one day the shooting started in New York between the MS-13 gang members and about twenty civilians in a neighborhood. The gang members broke into a home and killed the man, woman, and child that lived there. When they tried to leave the home the entire neighborhood opened fire on the gang members. Three of the gang members were killed with one wounded.

When the police got there the members of he neighborhood were all arrested for murder and he MS-13 gang members that survived were released. This mindset began to pop up all over he country and those living in the south were tired of all that was happening.

The Texas Governor was the first governor that made what was considered by the Liberal Communist as a declaration of war against those causing these problems. The list included all criminals and illegal aliens. Muslim Mosques were closed and Christian churches were reopened.

In many cases private citizens were picking up their rifles and fighting back at their local criminals. Piles of dead gang members and other known criminals were being found every day.

Not agreeing with this defiance of federal laws American soldiers were sent into Texas to gain control over the civil unrest but over ninety percent of them refused to fight other Americans.

After learning of this the president called in over 300,000 United Nations troops most of which went into Texas. Some surrounded Texas and remained in surrounding states. This caused these states to also rebel and fight these UN troops. Civil war was no longer just talked about. It had become fact.

January 7th was considered the official day that America's second civil war started. It was he day that the UN troops entered Texas. It was the day when the people fought back.

Scott Staninski was brought up on a small central Texas farm. He was twenty five years old and loved anything that kept him in the outdoors. After serving three years in the army as a sniper he decided to get out. Afghanistan and Iraq had to much desert sand for his liking and killing people did not set well in his heart either. So Scott did not reenlist.

He was allowed to carry his choice of rifles so, after checking many of them out he chose a Savage 270 rifle with a 6 x 32 scope. The bipod on the rifle extended out to twenty one inches so that he could fire from a sitting position. Laying on his stomach was painful. Scott combined his sniper skills with his love to hunt and kept his freezer full of fresh meat.

Scott was watching the news on his TV one night when they showed thousands of UN troops crossing the Oklahoma state line into Texas. When the reporter mentioned the words "civil war" Scott got up and got his gear ready to fight.

After his gear was ready Scott called a few of his friends. First he called Jerry, a man he met in Afghanistan. Only after fighting together for about a month did they finally realize that they're homes were only a few miles apart. Jerry had heard the news and was getting his gear together. He would be at Scott's home as soon as he could get there.

Next Scott called Bobby who he had gone to school with. Scott and Bobby met in the third grade and had been friends ever since. Next he called a two older friends that had been in the military many years ago.

Dave was an electrician in the air force for four years before getting out. Never seeing any action in the air force he was eager

to defend his sate of Texas. James had never been in the military but was very into the survival thing. Now facing defending his state he was ready for anything.

It took two hours for the four men to get to Scott's home. Scott had already been elected as their leader but there was no second in charge. After talking to the other four about this he chose Jerry because they had both seen action in Afghanistan. Bobby, Dave, and James had never seen any action and Scott needed someone that knew what it was like.

Now they had to plan what their next move would be. While they talked about it they continued to listen to the news on the TV. The reporter mentioned that many militias were forming all around the state of Texas and a few of them were close to Waco, Texas. However; Waco was a good forty miles away as the crow flies. Suddenly the TV went out. Then the men realized that all of the electrical things in Scott's home was off.

"The president must have turned off he electricity." Jerry mentioned.

Scott went into his back room and came back with a crank up AM/FM radio. After listening for a few minutes the person on the radio stopped talking and then mentioned that she was just informed that some of the electrical plants Around Texas had, had massive explosions and millions were without electricity. Then as the woman continued to speak even the radio went off and the ground started to shake a little. The men went outside and looked off to the west. High in the sky it was easy to see that there had been a very large explosion.

"My truck won't start." James yelled. The other men tried their trucks and they would not start either.

"EMP." Scott said. "Our lovable president has seen fit to knock out all of our electricity."

"You can bet that those Un troops have had their vehicles fixed to guard against the EMPs." Dave said.

"Maybe not." Bobby mentioned. "Remember a few minutes ago on the radio that woman said that the UN troops had stopped just inside the state line. Maybe this was why they stopped."

“Probably so then but … what do we do now?” Scott asked the others. “Should we join a militia or just remain as we are … our own group?”

“Our group does not even have a name.” James mentioned.

First the five men decided to stay as their own group. Then they decided on a name for their group. Although they expected to grow in numbers they would call themselves; The Savage Five.

The Savage Five would be a gorilla fighting type group. Because of the size of their group they would quickly hit the enemy and then run only to come back later and do it again. Now that they had decided on this and the name of the group where should they go?

“We could go to Waco and at least checkout the militia forming up there.” James suggested.

Dave and Bobby agreed so Scott took a vote. Everyone agreed to go and check things out. If anything they would learn where the fighting would be starting. The one thing that bothered Scott was that they would be fighting a better armed enemy with their hunting and semi-automatic rifles. They would have to grab fully automatic rifles when they could.

The walk to Waco would take three to four days so they would leave out early the next morning. For the rest of the day and into the night The Savage Five added bedrolls and food to their backpacks. Tents were out of the question because they were so bulky and heavy.

The next morning the five men got up at 0300 hours and started walking. Scot told the men that they would surely run into some kind of resistance so be ready to open fire if they felt they had to.

While The Savage Five were making their way to Waco they learned that three different militias were forming at the Waco stockyard. Scott knew where it was as he used to work there many years ago as a boy.

Three men that called themselves Generals were trying to form their own militias. Only one of them actually had any military experience. The other two were rich men that thought

that having money meant that they knew what they were doing.

General John Bolton had been a Marine for twenty years and a General for seven of those years. Mostly working behind the scene he had seen action in Afghanistan and Iraq. He and Scott had never met but Scott did serve under the General for a while. He was forming the 163rd Militia. He chose that number for the one hundred sixty three men that joined him before coming to Waco.

General Ted Newton was a spoilt rich boy with the emphasis on the word boy. Most of the men in Waco could see right through him but he was still collecting a few followers. He was forming the Newton Militia; named after himself.

General James Packard was another rich boy but at least he earned hisown money. He got rich after his construction company landed a state contract for rebuilding parts of Interstate 10. Soon after that he landed another contract with the state of Texas for rebuilding parts of Interstate 35 north of Waco. He still had no military experience but many of the men chose his militia over the Newton Militia. General Packard also named his militia after himself calling it the Packard Militia.

The Savage Five saw trouble only one time on their way to Waco. As they passed a home in Mart several people opened fire on them. None of them were hit but eleven others living there were killed. All of the dead men were black except for one. They called themselves The Black Militia.

The Black Militia had built a Mosque in the town and tried to force Shariah Law on the town. When they learned that the United Nations troops were coming into Texas they killed all of the police officers in Mart and were in the process of taking over the town when Scott and the others came through. Mostly made up of young boys and men they ran after loosing eleven of them to The Savage Five. They were not the men they thought that they were.

The next day the five men reached the stock yard just north of Waco. Thousands of me were already there.

"Check your radios and meet back here in two hours." Scott

ordered the others. Scott was a General Class HAM radio operator and had set the five of hem up with HAM handheld radios. Because he other four were not licensed operators they used the MUR frequencies which are used for training. Therefore anyone can talk on those frequencies. But to keep anyone else from hearing their conversations he had each channel set with a tone. Unless another person had that tone in their radio they would not hear any of the five talking. That day they were using channel one.

The five also had folding solar panels in their backpacks. It took two of these solar panels to recharge one of these radios. This was how they kept their radios charged on their trip to Waco.

For the next two hours the five men spread out and talked with many of he others there. The three Generals gave speeches in the auction room. Less than half of he men there could fit in the room but speakers were set up outside so the others could hear them speak. Finally it was time to regroup so Scott headed back outside.

After meeting together again everyone had a great deal to say. Each man spoke to the other four telling them what they had learned. Scott spoke last.

"Generals Newton and Packard are idiots ... rich boys that think they are leaders. I served under General Bolton in Afghanistan and I know him to be a good man and great leader. However; I am thinking of not joining any of these militias."

"Why not?" Bobby asked.

"We are not equipped to be fighting such well armed troops but we are equipped to fight so called Americans and Texans that are fighting against our freedom."

"You mean people like those Black Muslims in Mart?" Jerry asked.

"They would be a start." Scott suggested. "After freeing the town of Mart we can move on to other treasonist."

"I heard that Texas was going back to being called the Republic of Texas." James mentioned.

"One thing at a time guys." Scott said. "First ... what do you want to do?"

The five men talked for a while and decided to not join a militia. Then they voted to change the name of the group to The Texicans. All five agreed on this name. Then they talked about doing some recruiting while they were there. They needed more men so the five agreed to do it. By the end of the day the Texicans had fourteen men and three woman wanting to join them.

The Texicans pitched a camp just down the road little and interviewed those wanting to join. Those wanting to join told the five why they wanted to join and what they had to offer the group. By midnight the five had settled on twelve men and all three of the women. The others were asked to leave camp.

Jerry was second in charge so Scott made Bobby and Dave lieutenants and placed eight of the men under Bobby and the remaining men and the women under Dave. Lieutenant Bobby Davis was over Fire Team 1 and Lieutenant Dave Tailor was in charge of Fire Team 2. James did not want to lead in any way so Scott made him a Sergeant directly under him. James was more of a scavenger and he was good at it.

The group was now low on food so James' first job was to find some food. At the feed store next door he found some corn and started to bring it back when he saw two large plastic jars of Chia seeds. When he brought the Chia seeds into the camp the group considered shooting him. James mixed some of the Chia seeds in some warm water and let it set for a few minutes. Then he allowed everyone in he group try it.

The seeds had built up a slim and the seeds themselves were still a little crunchy. Then James added sugar to the mixture and they all tried it again.

"The Chia seeds are filling but there is no nutrition in them. That is why you add sugar to it ... to make it taste better and to give you the energy you need. You can even add some cocoa mix for a chocolate flavor."

After that everyone started listening to James a little more. He had been into survival foods for many years and this was just one of his ideas. He was the perfect person for being their scavenger.

With The Texicans being twenty strong they left the Waco stock yard and headed for the town of Mart. Their first job would be to free the town of the Black Muslim group that had killed all of their police and taken over the town.

That night they camped in a field not to far from the town. Still being far enough away from the town so that their gunfire would not be heard Scott send out two men to do some hunting. They came back three hours later with three rabbits. That night hey would have meat; not much but still some.

The three cotton tail rabbits were small but all cotton tails are. After being cleaned the rabbits were hung from small tree limbs cut just for cooking them. A fourth small limb had many tiny limbs which held the rabbit's livers and hearts.

All twenty of the Texicans ate but no one got full. This would become a way of like for them from then on. Food would become hard to find and very expensive if it was even found. They all slept a few hours. Around midnight Scott woke everyone up to get closer to the town before daylight. Almost six hours later they stood in a field of high grass just west of Mart. From there they watched the town to see what the Black Muslims were doing. They would move into the town that night.

Only being able to see the western end of town the Texicans watch the town of Mart all day. They witnessed three different times men being marched out into the street and being executed; shot for one reason or another. Other gunshots were heard farther into town during the day but the Texicans could not see that far. Finally it got dark enough and the Texicans moved into the town.

As the group took their time walking into the town they heard voices at the grain silos. Sticking close to the buildings and bushes the group worked their way to the silos and found about fifteen of he Black Muslims drinking. The men were young with the oldest looking to be only about nineteen years old.

"I thought that Muslims didn't drink." Jerry whispered to

Scott.

"They don't. Scott quietly replied. "These are not true Muslims. They're just using the Muslim religion to justify what they are doing."

"So we will not be killing real Muslims then." Jerry said.

Jerry had two friends that were Muslim and they were good people. It bothered him to just go after Muslims but now they would not be doing that.

Scott called for nine of the Texicans to get closer to him. Then he ordered Jerry to take the nine and attack the young men with sudden force. Then they were to retreat back to him.

Jerry kept the others close to him as they sneaked closer to the group of young men. Then he gave the order to attack and the nine Texicans ran in and started to fire but no one fired. None of the Black Muslims were holding any weapons.

"Hold your fire." Jerry said as he walked into the lights.

Suddenly three of the young men grabbed rifles that they had leaning against that one silo and opened fire. The nine had no problem firing then. In just a few seconds the firing was over and all the young Black Muslims were dead. Two of the Texicans were also dead and one was wounded. Scott and the others that stayed behind walked up to Jerry and the nine.

"What happened?" Scott asked Jerry.

"I didn't see them holding any weapons so we didn't fire." Jerry defended his decision. "Then suddenly the shooting started and we ..."

"You hesitated and got two men killed and another one wounded that might die." Scott snapped. Scott put his hand on his friend's shoulder and added; "Try to do better next time."

"Yes Sir." Jerry calmly agreed.

The Texicans spent the next six hours working their way through the town only having to fight three times. As they worked their way through the town they encouraged the townspeople to come out and help free their town. By time the Texicans had worked their way to the east end of town almost two hundred of the townspeople were with them. Any Black

Muslims that were left in town were in hiding or running.

The townspeople thanked the Texicans as they walked back to the western end of town. The wounded man had been shot in the chest and died of his wounds. The town offered to bury the three dead men so that the Texicans could fallow three of the Black Muslims south towards Marlin. There was believed to be another larger group of Black Muslims in Marlin.

After loosing three men the Texicans only had seventeen left. Before leaving Mart Scot asked for volunteers to join their small militia. Scott and the other original four Savage Five interviewed many of the young headwomen wanting to join the Texicans. By morning they had settled on twenty two from the town; sixteen men and six women. The Texicans were now thirty nine strong.

Scott gave a speech to the new members of the Texicans and made sure that they knew their chain of command. Then he gave three volunteers to James to help him in any scavenging. He split the remaining new people between Bobby and Dave. Their Fire Teams had grown to two squads each.

Scott organized the people of the town. After getting their rifles and shotguns back from the Black Muslims they would be able to defend themselves. From then on they would keep their weapons loaded and ready to fight. Noon was going to takeover their town again and the Texans were welcomed back anytime.

Because everyone had been up all night Scott decided to wait until the next morning before moving onto Marlin. The people of Mart ransacked the homes of the Black Muslims that were there and gave everything to the Texicans. That day they ate their fill of roasted chicken and other things that had been taken from the people. The people of the town were so thankful that they showered the Texicans with food, wine, and even a little moonshine. Finally Scott had to asked them to allow the Texicans to rest so they could leave out the next morning.

That night Scott had guards set out to watch the area in case the Black Muslims came back with help. For the first time since leaving their homes Scott got some well deserved rest.

The next morning Bobby woke up Scott and the others. He

had, had the watch from midnight till morning while training some of the newer members of the Texicans. Scott wanted to leave Mart before the people of the town got there to see them off. He knew that they would slowdown their leaving and he wanted to do most of their walking before it got to warm. Before the sun even came up the Texicans were on their way to Marlin.

Chapter 2

El Diablo

The Texicans spent that night in a large field with high grass. They had plenty offered and dried fruit so there was no need for a fire. Before turning in to get some sleep Scott walked out into the field to get away from the others.

"Father … I'm sorry I haven't prayed in so long. Not once since leaving my home have I asked for your help and yet … you were right there helping me anyway. Now we are heading to Marlin … a town that is spread out and they have more of these Black Muslims than Mart did. I don't know how to handle this new threat Father. Please go with us and help us to save the new Republic of Texas. Thank you Father. Amen."

Scott turned to go back to the camp when he found one of the new members from Mart standing in front of him.

"Oh I'm sorry Sir." the woman said. "I'm standing watch out here and came to see who was out here. When I heard you praying I stayed quiet until you finished."

"No problem …" Scott said. "What's your name?"

"I'm Private Deacon … Evie Deacon Sir."

"Well Private … you did good." Never interrupt me while I'm talking to our Lord unless you have to. I'm pretty sure that God won't care then."

"You know Sir … Robert E. Lee prayed every day asking God's help." Deacon said. "It feels good to know that the man I am fallowing also prays."

Private Deacon continued her walking around on watch while Scott returned to the camp. I minutes he was off to sleep. During the night he had a dream in which he was in the civil war.

Then he saw that he was Robert E. Lee. When the dream was over he was being awaken to get ready to leave out again. He wondered if he had he dream because Private Deacon mentioned Robert E. Lee or was God showing him that he would be the next leader in this new American civil war. He got up and readied his gear smiling all the while. He liked the idea of being a great leader but he also knew that he was just a simple man.

Some people like Robert E. Lee become great leaders after years of training for it and people have greatness thrust upon them. Scott was one of those that greatness would have to be thrust upon him. He was not trained for it.

The next evening the Texicans came within one mile of Marlin. Scotts had Dave send two of his men closer to check things out. Using Dave's radio they reported back that General Bolton's 163rd Militia was there so Scott and the others went on into town.

Scott found the General and walked up to him. "General Bolton Sir."

"Yes." the General said. "I was with you in Afghanistan a few years ago as a sniper."

"I never met all of the men under me but I'm happy to see that you made it home." the General said. "Many did not."

"Yes Sir." Scott commented. "I lost a sniper friend tannery sniper."

"Sorry Son." the General said. "What can I do for you?"

"We just came up from Mart to take care of the Black Muslim group here in Marlin." Scott told the General. "I had no idea as to how we were going to do it. Sure glad to see you all here."

"You just came up out of Mart?" the General asked.

"Yes Sir." Scott admitted. "My group … The Texicans … wiped out the Black Muslims there and set the town free."

"Yes." the General said with a big smile. We captured three of them coming here to join the Muslims here so I heard what you all did. Great job."

"Thank you Sir."

"Who are you with?" the General asked.

"No one Sir. We are our own group." Scott admitted.

"I don't like that."

"Well I'm sorry Sir." Scott said. "But we are going to stay our own group ... The Texicans."

"To bad." the General admitted. "I could use a group of fighters like yours."

"We are not interested infighting UN troops Sir." Scott informed the General. "Our goal is to get rid of those that fight against us. We want to wipe any and all resistance for a free Republic of Texas."

The General looked at Scott and said; "I guess you haven't heard."

"Haven't heard what Sir?" Scott asked.

"The UN troops are moving out of Texas." the General advised. "The president has given Texas and California to Mexico. Their troops are suppose to cross the border into Texas next week."

"Well actually that's better." Scott admitted. "I have no problem shooting Mexicans trying to take our state."

"We are heading to the border in hopes of getting close enough to make a difference." the General said. "You all want to join us?"

"No tank you Sir." Scott reluctantly said. He felt bad but he and the others had already made up their minds.

"Oh by the way." the General advised. We took care of the Black Muslims here so you can move on to your next goal. Good luck ..." The general thought for a second and then asked; "What rank are you?"

"I have no rank Sir." Scott advised. "I'm just the leader of the Texicans."

"What is the highest rank in your group?"

"I have two Lieutenants." Scott was not sure what the General was getting at.

"Then if you don't mind I'm making you a Captain ... not in my militia but just your own."

My own group?" Scott asked.

"No." the General said. "Your own militia. I'm considering your group the Texican Militia. I look forward to working with you someday." The General started to leave and then whipped around and added; "By the way Captain ... I was wrong about you. I do like what your doing."

With that General Bolton moved on to take care of some things before the 163rd Militia headed out to the south.

Scot went back to the others and told them what had happened. They talked it over and excepted the name Texican Militia. They also excepted Scott as being a Captain. Scott made Jerry a first Lieutenant and Bobby and Dave Second Lieutenants. Against James' will Scott made him a Second Lieutenant as well.

Scott then asked the Texicans exactly what they wanted to do. Jerry wanted to wipe out the illegal population in the area but Dave called it murder. For a long time they discussed it and finally agreed on attacking only illegal aliens from countries south of the Republic of Texas. But for the most part they would concentrate on ridding the Republic of Texas of all Liberal/Communist. It was their Liberal Socialist Communist president that caused this whole problem.

The Texicans drew a new line in the sand and they had no desire to be nice about it. Scott got word that a few of the Black Muslims from Marlin ran to the east so the Texicans would be heading east next. But for now they would rest the night and leave out just before daylight next morning.

Scott was warming up a can of soup when another Texican walked up to him and said; "I don't think we need to go after those men tomorrow."

"And you are who?" Scott asked.

"I'm Private Don Mickey." the man said. "I joined your group backing Mart."

"Okay Private ... why do you think we should not go after them?" Scott always listened to others. He always thought that they might have a better idea.

"They are only three men." the Private advised. "What can they do?"

"Private Mickey." Scott said with a firm voice. "Right now we do not have any other pressing issues to fallow or enemies to chaise other than these three men. And you don't know what kind of trouble they will cause when they get to the next town."

"That would be Kosse Sir." Dave mentioned.

"That's right Lieutenant. Thank you."

Well ... I just don't think we should go after them." Private Mickey said again.

"Lieutenant." Scott said to Dave hoping that he would take control of the Private.

"Private." Dave said. "The Captain appreciates your input but he does make the final decisions around here.. We fallow his orders not yours."

"I'm sorry Sir." the private said as he turned and walked away.

"Gutsy little guy isn't he." Bobby said.

"He's just green." Scott said.

"Aren't we all?" Jerry asked.

The next morning the Texicans got up early and left west Marlin before daylight. By time they got to the far eastern part of the town it was almost 1000 hours. Highway 7 was covered with people trying to make it to safer places.

Everyone knew that the president had abandoned Texas and gave Texas and California to Mexico. Governor Davis continued to govern the new Republic of Texas as President but only until the fighting was over and an election could decide on a president.

It was late September when the Texican Militia walked into the town of Kosse. As soon as the stepped into town Scott had the others spread out. He did not want everyone grouped together in case they were ambushed. As the Texicans walked through the town people that saw them quickly went into their homes. There were many gangs out and no one knew who to trust.

What Scott and the other Texicans did not know was that a platoon of soldiers from Mexico had moved into the area. Their job was to get as far north as they could and cause as much havoc as they could giving the regular Mexican army time to move across the border. When the Mexican platoon saw the Texicans walking up they street in Kosse they decided to make their stand there.

Before Scott and the others knew that anyone was even watching them four explosions went off killing at least seven of the Texicans. Then gunfire opened up down the street killing and wounding another four of them. The Texicans scattered and opened fire on those down the street that were firing at them.

Suddenly another explosion went off sending Scott into the side of a building. For a second or two he looked around and then passed out. When Scott woke up it was dark. He had been passed out all day.

As Scott tried to move he found pieces o boards and bricks on top of him. A large piece of tin lay across him as well. Not knowing if anyone was still around he slowly moved out from under the debris. As he got to his knees he looked around and found no one standing around. He stood and looked around for any of the Texicans that might be there.

After a while he found twenty nine members of his militia dead. Eight men and two of the women were missing. Jerry, Bobby, and Dave were among the dead. Two of the women were also dead but he did not find Evie, Lea, and Don. He found one AR-15 under some rubble and picked it up. It had a full thirty round magazine in it.

As he started to walk away he almost tripped over a pipe. As he looked down he saw that the pipe was really his 270 rifle. Hoping that the scope was still set he shouldered the rifle and stepped into the shadows. Looking around for a while he tried to guess where the other Texicans might be. They had to have been captured but where were they taken?

As Scott looked around he heard the muffled sound of what sounded like a women trying to scream. Just a few feet awaya Mexican soldier was dragging a woman around he building and into the darkness where he was. Scott pulled his dagger and leaned his AR-15 against the building. When the man got closer Scott grabbed him with his left hand and swung him around. Then he stabbed the Mexican soldier three time in the back puncturing the man's heart twice.

Then Scott realized that he woman was Evie of his Texican Militia. "Evie?"he asked.

"Scott" Evie said as she gave him a big hug.

"Where are the others?" Scott wasted no time asking.

"They're in a home around the corner." Evie said. "Scott." she said stopping him as he turned to walk towards the home. "There're the Mexican army."

"Who is?" Scott asked.

"The men that attacked us and took the others prisoner." she advised him. "They aren't just a bunch of Mexicans with guns. There're the Mexican army."

"How many are there?"

"About twenty I guess." she replied. We killed some of them in that fight but there are still about twenty left."

Scott thought for a moment and then changed rifles with Evie. Then he went back to the dead and found three more AR-15 magazines. Unloading one of them he was able to fill the other two. He now had three, fully loaded thirty round magazines.

"You take the 270 and get across he street." he told Evie. "After I start shooting you shoot anyone of those Mexican bastards you see coming out the backdoor."

"What are you going to do?" Evie asked.

Scott looked into Evie's eyes and said; "I'm getting my people back."

When Scott walked up to the front door of the home he saw two of the Mexican soldiers sanding outside. Two quick shots took them out. It was quiet in the home and then the other soldiers started laughing. They thought that their friend had killed Evie.

Scott slowly opened the front door to the home and then slung it open. Then he started firing at anything wearing a brown uniform until the magazine was empty. He quickly loaded

another magazine in his rifle and continued to fire. Some of the soldiers were almost killing each other trying to get out of the two broken windows but Scott just filled the openings with their bodies.

When the second magazine was empty he pushed he release button dropping the empty magazine to the floor. After loading the last of his magazines he continued to fire. When that magazine was empty he dropped the rifle and pulled his dagger again. Then he went to work with it.

Only two of the Mexican soldiers remained and they were stuck in the window. "Los Diablo" they both kept yelling. Then they both flouted the window and ran off into the darkness.

"Anybody back there?" Scott asked. Seconds later James stuck his head around the corner and then came out.

The others fallowed James into the den. The floor was so cluttered with dead Mexicans that everyone moved outside. Evie crossed the street and joined the group.

"Did you hear what those two Mexicans were calling you?" Evie asked Scott.

"No." he said as he seemed to be in shock. "No I didn't."

"They were yelling El Diablo … The Devil." she told him. "They thought you were the devil that had come after them."

"I'm a Christian." Scott insisted. I don't want to be called the devil."

"You don't understand Sir." Evie said. "They were scared to death. Calling you the devil was actually a sign of respect. From now on any Mexicans that hear that you're around … that the devil is around will also be scared to death.

Evie was right. The two Mexican soldiers that got away told heir friends later that the devil came for them and they could not kill him. Within weeks of that night fear filled the hearts of every illegal Mexican in Texas.

The Texican Militia now had just eight men and two women. Scott was not sure if he wanted the Texicans to grow anymore or if he wanted to just be alone. He considered going alone with his 270 rifle as a gorilla fighter. From a far distance he would hit

targets, retreat, and then go back and hit more targets. However; he still had eight men and two women left so, for the time being he would keep the militia going.

But being alone for so long was not something he looked forward to. Scott was also starting to like Evie. Many times they would talk, sometimes late into the night. Although Evie never said so he felt that she liked him as well.

Scott and the others went back to where the Mexicans attacked the Texicans. They drug their friends out from under the boards and broken bricks and buried them a in a grassy area a few feet from the silos. Then they collected all of the rifles and magazines and kept the ones that had not been destroyed in the many explosions.

The Texican Militia spent the night close to their buried friends. They worked on their rifles and magazines and got some well deserved rest. They would leave out early the next morning.

As UN troops lined the Texas borders with New Mexico, Oklahoma, Arkansas, and Louisiana those states rebelled and started fighting the UN troops. The National Guard units in those states did not fight long before the UN troops left their borders with Texas. After that the US president spread the UN troops throughout the rest of the United States.

California was in the process of being taken over by the Mexican government. With the state being full of pacifist Liberal the people of California did not resist. The entire state was taken over within one week.

Because American soldiers refused to fight other Americans the US president had UN troops take over all military bases. Then they kicked out all American soldiers and captured all weaponry and ammunition.

The Texican Militia moved out of Kosse towards Groesbeck. One of the people living in Kosse said that they saw the two Mexican soldiers running in that direction. However; no one remembered seeing three young black men coming into the town the past couple of days. Not knowing which direction they went there was no way to fallow. Now they had a new target that meant more to them than the three Black Muslims. The young Muslims were just Americans that chose the wrong side. The Mexican soldiers were the enemy; invaders of their new republic. Scott wanted them before they joined up with any other Mexican soldiers that may have come this far into Republic of Texas now called the RoT.

Two days later the Texican Militia reached the small town of Thorton located halfway between Kosse and Groesbeck. The town was actually just over the railroad tracks on the east side of Highway 14. Scott stood on Highway 14 and looked at the town across the railroad tracks. The other Texicans were scattered behind him.

There were no other major roads leading off of Highway 14 before getting there so the two Mexican soldiers had to be there. Scott saw no movement in the town until a man waved at him. Just over the railroad tracks was a wall made of crushed cars. Behind the wall were few men of the town. They were all armed.

"Keep moving on down the road." the man behind the wall of cars yelled.

"We're the Texican Militia and we are ..." Scott said before being interrupted.

"What ever you have we don't want it." the man yelled again.

"May I come over there and talk to you?" Scott yelled.

The man talked with the therewith him and then yelled back; "Lay your rifle down and come alone."

Scott lay his rifle on the highway and then raised his hands to show that he was unarmed. Then he started walking and met the man on the Railroad tracks.

As Scott reached the man he stuck out his hand and said; I'm Captain Staninski of the Texican Militia."

"Not many of you for a militia." the man said. "My name is Jordon."

"We had a fight in Kosse with a platoon of Mexican soldiers." Scott said. "They killed over half of my people and now we are chasing two of them."

"We saw two men yesterday wearing brown uniforms."

Jordon said. “Was that them?”

“Yes.” Scott admitted. “Where are they?”

“They just kept walking past us towards Groesbeck.” Jordon told Scott. “The Mexicans have already made it up this far north?”

“Just one platoon but … we wiped them out except for two of them. We’ve chased them here.”

“Well they kept going to Groesbeck so we didn’t say anything to them.” Jordon said.

Scott thanked Jordon for talking with him and shook his hand. Then he walked back to the others. After telling the other Texicans what he learned they continued their walk to Groesbeck. That night they set up camp on the side of Highway 14 just four miles from Groesbeck. They next cay they would walk into the town of Groesbeck and try to find the two Mexican soldiers.

The next day just before noon the Texican Militia walked into the outskirts of Groesbeck. Suddenly they found themselves surrounded by many men and women with rifles. Outnumbered at least two to one the Texican Militia was ordered to lay down their weapons. Scott told the others to obey. Four vans drove up and the Texicans were loaded into them. Their firearms were loaded into a pick-up truck. Then they were all taken to the Limestone County Jail.

Chapter 3

The EMP Guns

The vans pulled around to the back of the jail. Minutes later the back doors to the vans were opened and the Texicans were unloaded. They were stood against the wall of the jail and ordered to their knees. One by one they were taken inside where're were searched and placed in cells.

Suddenly Scot heard a voice behind him. "You the leader?"

"Yes." Scot kept it short and sweet.

A few seconds later Scott was stood and taken inside. He was not placed in a cell but a room where an older man was waiting for him. After being pushed down into a chair across the table from the old man he was asked who he and the others were.

Scott talked with the old man for a while and learned that they were only taken into custody because the guards did not know who they were. The old man left the room and Scott sat there with two armed men behind him. A few minutes later the old man came back and said that they were going to be released. Instantly Scott asked the old man about the two Mexican soldiers. They had not seen any Mexican soldiers.

The Texicans were given a hot meal in a locked cellblock emptied so they could be put there. Scott was taken to the sheriff's office where he met the Sheriff himself. They talked for a while and then Scott was taken to the others. About an hour later the Texicans were taken back outside where they had come in. The pick-up truck with their weapons was there and they were allowed to get what was taken from them.

The Texican Militia was taken to the eastern side of Groesbeck about half a mile from the jail and released. Then the Sheriff ordered them not to return to Groesbeck.

"We are fighting for you ... you bastard." Scott told the

Sheriff. "It's not like you're doing any fighting you old coot."

The Sheriff smiled and politely asked Scot to take his militia out of their area. Then the Sheriff got back in his truck and his driver drove off. Five men stood behind railroad crossties stacked into a wall. All of the Texicans were mad at how they were treated but Scott saw a no win situation.

"Okay ... let's get out'a here." Scott ordered the others. After one final nasty look at the guards Scott turned and led the Texican Militia east towards the town of Donnie.

It took three days to reach the town of Donnie. Someone had blown up two of the bridges on State Highway 164 This caused them to had to look for another way around the crumbled concrete and rebar.

As the Texicans rounded the curve in the highway they could see a little ways into the small town of Donnie. Smoke was rising from some of the buildings and many of the citizens were busy at cleaning up the town. Someone had attacked the town and then left before finishing the job and taking over the town. As the Texicans walked into town women started screaming. Men and women started running for their lives. A few of the people started shooting at Scott and the others.

"Hold your fire." Scott yelled. The shooting stopped. "I'm Captain Staninski of the Texican Militia." We are not your enemy."

A few of he men that had been firing at the Texicans stepped out and met Scott in the street. As the men and women of the town of Donnie talked with the Texicans Scott learned that another platoon of Mexican soldiers had hit the town the night before. Short of actually taking the town they stopped firing, marched through town and left for the town of Buffalo.

Scott also learned that the Mexican platoon had seven trailers pulled behind Humvees. These trailers had to have been full of weapons and explosives. The people of Donnie were so appreciative of the Texicans that they fed them that night and allowed them to spend the night there. The best thing about the town was that they had thirteen young men and women that joined the Texican Militia. The militia now had eighteen men and five women.

With it starting to get colder many of the people donated blankets, jackets, and sleeping bags to the Texicans. It was early October and although the first cold snap had not hit the nights were still cold.

That night two men walked into the Texican camp wanting to talk to Scott. The three men sat around the campfire as Scott listened to what the two men had to say. As the two men told Scott about the Mexicans he realized that there had been an EMP blast. *Then what was that large flash in the sky back at his home?* He asked himself. *How did that flash coincide with all electrical things no longer working?*

Scott was finding more mysteries than answers with these two men. So if there was no EMP Blast then what could be wrong with the electricity? The two men went on to say that they had heard that the Mexicans had a device on a trailer that emitted an EMP Blast in a particular direction at a maximum rang of about five to ten miles. Just two or three or these things could wipe out the electrical grid for many miles around while leaving other areas unaffected. This was how the UN and Mexican troops and their vehicles were able to continue running.

Armed with this new information the Texicans had a new mission. After the two men left Scott had a talk with the other Texicans. He told them what the two men said about the EMP Guns. They were not actually guns as much as an EMP emitter. No matter what their names were the Texican Militia was still going after them. The next morning the Texicans left Donnie for the town of Buffalo.

As the Texican Militia walked out of town many of the people cheered them on. The people of Donnie saw them as heroes while the people of Groesbeck saw them as a group of unruly freedom fighters with little or no leadership. Scott saw this and realized that they would not be welcomed everyplace they went.

The two men said that the Mexican military took the three EMP Guns towards Buffalo so the Texican Militia would go there. However; there was still one question that bothered Scott. Was the story that the two men told him even true. He would know for sure by time they got to Buffalo.

The Texican Militia took Highway 164 towards Buffalo. They were only three miles out of Donnie when a group of men opened fire on them from the tree line on both sides of the road. Who ever it was had them in a crossfire and they were out in the open with nothing to hide behind. Suddenly Scott was hit and he went down.

When Scott woke up he was falling through a tunnel. Millions of arms were reaching out of the wall of the tunnel trying to grab him. Other people were in the tunnel as well and every now and then one of the hands would grab them and pull them in to the wall where they would disappear.

Then suddenly one of the hands grabbed Scott. He fought hard to get away but he could not escape the grip of the red scaly hand. That was when Scott found himself falling into a large underground cavern. Ashe continued to fall he saw that much of the flood of the cavern was covered in flames. The air was hot and sticky. When he hit the floor he quickly stood wondering how he survived the fall.

Suddenly a hand grabbed his arm. As he looked to see who it was he realized that the hand belonged to a creature that stood at least a foot over him. The creature was large and had red scales that covered its body. It was unbelievably strong. The creature looked at him and growled. Then it threw him at least thirty feet. The pain in his arm was great. As he looked at his arm he saw that it was not broken. Before he could stand another creature grabbed his arm and picked him up.

This creature looked much like the first one but it did not have scales. The skin on this creature seemed to be rotting and the smell of rotting flesh fill the hot thin air. Scott could hardly breath. Like with the first creature this one looked at Scott and growled. Then it also threw him.

This time Scott landed in a small pit of flames. He screamed as his flesh melted from his body. Slowly he crawled out of the pit

of fire and onto the smoking black rock. It was also hot but not as hot as the flames. Mustering all of the strength he could he got to his knees and looked up.

"I thought I was a Christian Father. What have I done to deserve this?"

Another creature grabbed Scott and squeezed him until his intestines almost came up his throat. As this creature held onto him smaller creatures about eight to ten inches tall jumped on him and began to bite. Blood poured from the bites and the pain was more than he could bare.

This went on for about an hour when Scott saw that he was floating upward. Ten he was backing the tunnel with hands reaching out to grab him but, none could grab him. Far ahead on him in the tunnel he could see a light. *Could this be the end of the tunnel?* he thought to himself. *Would the tunnel open up back in hell where he was? Could he be going to a hotter hell; maybe a worse hell that where he was?*

Suddenly without any warning Scott flew out of the tunnel and landed of soft grass. He looked at his arms and saw that his skin was back to normal. After standing he first noticed that the air was cool and refreshing. Then he saw a small bridge in front of him.

The bridge crossed a creak that was no more than two feet wide. He could easily just step over the creak but he had such an urge to use the bridge. However; standing on the bridge was what looked like an angel. The angel's hands rested on the handle of a large sword. The point of the sword rested on the bridge between the angel's feet. The handle of the sword where the angel's hands rested came up to the angel's mouth. The angel was wearing an all white robe tied just above the waist with a white cotton rope.

"May I pass?" Scott asked the angel.

"Not yet." the angel said.

"Then ... when?" Scott asked again.

"You may cross when he gets here." the angel advised.

Scott looked behind him and saw that the tunnel was gone. When he looked back at the bridge he saw that the angel had moved to the side of the bridge and beside him stood a man also dressed in a white robe. A bright light emitted from this second man so bright that Scot could not look directly at his face.

Scott was lead across the bridge and up a shallow hill to a city that also shined so brightly that Scott could not see well. As they walked the man introduced himself as Jesus. Instantly Scot fell to the ground crying but Jesus picked him up. The closer that they got to the city the easier it became to see around.

As Scott walked up to the gate of the city Jesus told him; "You may not enter the city yet. Your time has not yet come. But there are others here that want to see you." Scott would later describe the voice of Jesus as being a deep voice.

The first person that walked up to Scott was his grandfather. Then other family members took their time talking to him. Then a young lady walked up to Scott and described herself as his unborn daughter. A few years earlier he had talked his girl friend into having an abortion and this young lady was that aborted child. Again Scott fell to his knees.

"Forgive me for what I did." Scott cried out but the young lady picked him up and gave him a hug.

"It's okay Dad. I still love you." the young lady told him.

Suddenly a peace came over Scott and he found himself back at the entrance of the tunnel. He looked behind him and saw that the angel was back on duty on the bridge. Then a voice came out from everywhere and Scott knew that it was God.

"It's not your time yet Scott and you have other things to do." the voice rang out from all around. "I am going to make you a great man; a great leader of your people. Sometimes you will need to be vicious but other time I need you to be merciful. Do you understand?"

"Yes Father." Scott said.

"Your militia will grow." the voice said. "You will lead others into battle but my hand will be upon you. No one will be able to take your life."

When Scott opened his eyes he was laying in the middle of Highway 164. Three of the other Texicans were dead in the middle of the road. The others had been captured and were being tied not far from him. The men that had captured them were all wearing brown uniforms. None of the Mexicans saw Scott standing.

When Scot was standing he looked at the Mexicans who had just noticed him. For a while the just stood there and did not move. Then one of the Mexicans moved and Scott started firing an AR-15 that he had picked up. Within seconds twelve of the Mexicans were dead and three others were surrendering. "El Diablo." they yelled as they fell to their knees and begged for mercy.

Some of the Texicans started to shoot the three Mexicans but Scott yelled out and stopped them. As Scott slowly walked up to the Mexicans one passed out from fear. The other two continued to beg for mercy.

Neither of the two Mexicans spoke any English so Scott sent them on their way. They would later tell others about this newest attack of El Diablo. When they ran off the other Mexican woke up. Seeing that his friends were gone he thought that El Diablo had sent them to Hell. Still on his knees he continued to beg for mercy.

"Please Diablo. Spare my life."

"I will spare your life if you stop calling me Diablo." Scott said.

"You're not … the devil?"

"No." Scott insisted. "I am only a soldier like you."

"Then why are you showing me any mercy?" the Mexican asked."

"Because God told me to." Scott answered him.

The Mexican thought for a moment and then asked; "May I still fallow you?"

"But we are the enemy."

"You're not my enemy anymore." the Mexican soldier advised. "Please let me fallow you."

"We could use an interpreter ." James said.

Scott thought for a moment and then walked a shot distance down the road to pray.

"I am doing what you wanted but this man will not leave. What should I do Lord?"

Scott took in a deep breath and then the thought cam to his mind. *I sent this man to you.*

Scott went back to the others and asked the soldier his name. He called himself Sergeant Julio Sanchez. Julio was born in Brownsville and had lived there all his life. That was how he spoke such good English. When the war started he moved to Mexico and joined the Mexican military. After a two week boot camp he was made a Sergeant and was sent across the border into Texas.

Julio would not be allowed to carry a firearm and he would be watched. The Texican Militia spent the night on the bank of a creak which gave them water for cooking and coffee. They had one campfire but set out two guards at all times keeping their eyes up and down the Highway.

As Scott sat by the campfire Evie walked up and sat beside him. "I saw your head after you went down." Evie said. "I did not see the little scratch that I see now. What happened?"

Scott told Evie what happened to him. He told her about going to Hell and then to Heaven. Then he told her what God said to him just before leaving Heaven. "He told me that I would have to be vicious but, he also wanted me to be merciful when I could."

"Is that why you let the other two Mexican soldiers go free?" she asked.

Evie moved against Scott, wrapped her arm around his and then lay her head on his shoulder. "I'm glad you're a man that does what God wants."

The next morning the Texicans got up long before daylight and got on their way. Julio was walking beside Scott when he suddenly threw his arm in front of Scott and whispered; "Stop

Sir." They were still a good mile from the town of Buffalo.

Scott threw up his right fist signaling to the others behind him to stop.

"What is it?" Scott asked Julio.

"I don't know Sir." Julio said. "Something isn't right."

Just as Julio said that gunfire opened up in Buffalo. They were still a mile from the outskirts of the town so Scott had the others spread out and fallow him. Double timing it to Highway 75 they were all now to tired to fight. Scott looked back at the others and saw them gasping for air. He had made mistake running them to that spot. He ordered them all to the side of the buildings until they were ready to move on.

Just as the Texicans hunkered against the side of the buildings Scott looked up the highway and saw about thirty Mexican soldiers retreating from who ever it was that was fighting them. He gave orders to open fire on the Mexicans. Within seconds every Mexican soldier that was in retreat was dead.

Scott stepped out on the side of he highway and looked ahead. He could see many men standing in the middle of he highway looking at them. Then one of them raised a hand and waved. Scott waved back and started walking towards those up the road.

After talking to the men in town that had been fighting the Mexican soldiers Scott realized that this was General Ted Newton's Militia. Newton was the General he disliked the most. However; the men under him seemed to be great fighters. Not many of them had any respect for him as a leader though.

Darren was one of these men. Scott learned a great deal from Darren as they talked. He took Scott to the General who was sitting in his tent at a folding table writing.

"General Sir." Darren said as he pulled back the flap on the General's tent. Captain Scott Staninski to see you Sir."

General Newton stood and stuck out his hand. "Heard a lot about you ... El Diablo."

"I don't really care for that name Sir." Scott said.

“Don’t be silly Captain.” the General commented. “Your small militia has put more fear in the enemy’s heart than I ever will.”

The two men talked for a long time. The General had not heard about any EMP guns and said that no Mexican machinery of any type came through Buffalo. Scott had wondered if he story about the EMP guns was true but for the first time he really thought that he was fallowing a lie. But why would that man have lied to him about this?

“I was fallowing that story too.” the General said. “I heard in Jewett that the EMP guns were but when we got here we only found about one company of Mexican soldiers.”

“How many Mexican soldiers have made it this far north?” Scott asked.

“I got word from Central Command in Dallas that six or seven battalions forced their way into the Republic of Texas.” the General said. These battalions are mostly from Mexico but some of them are from other South American countries.”

“What is this Central Command in Dallas?” Scott asked.

General Newton laughed and then said; “You really need to keeping touch with what is going on.”

Scott put his hand on the long knife hanging from his side and asked; “How would you like for me to cut that smirk off of your face?”

The General stopped laughing. “Now, now my friend. We should not be fighting each other.”

“Please answer the question … Sir.” Scott was trying to be respectful even if he did have no respect for the General.

“Dallas is what we call Free Texas. With most of he Texas National Guard on the borders with other states watching the UN troops watching us … Dallas and Fort Worth are free cities. The Central Command is based in Dallas and they giveus our orders.”

“No one gives me orders.” Scott insisted. “The members of the Texican Militia vote on many things with me as their leader. I make final decisions.”

“And as you go gallivanting around you get in our way.”

General Newton said with a hint of anger in his voice.

Scott stood and said; "You're nothing but a spoilt rich boy with the emphasis on the word boy. Because you were born into money you think you should command men. You may have run some company before shit hit the fan but you're an ass with no military experience." Scott turned to walk out of the tent but turned around and added; "You need to stay out of my way."

As Scott walked back to the other Texicans many of the men in Newton's Militia talked with him. They overheard Scott's yelling at General Newton and had been looking for a way to leave the militia. They begged Scott to allow them to join the Texican Militia.

Scott stopped and looked at the men. "Go get your things and meet me at our camp. But hurry. We're leaving very soon."

When Scott got to the Texican camp he ordered everyone to get ready to move out. A few minutes later other men from Newton's Militia started walking into the camp. After warning the new men that Julio was with them they all left camp and headed back towards Donnie. After they were three miles from Buffalo the Texicans stopped and rested until morning. Scott just wanted to getaway from General Newton.

One of the men built a campfire and Scott found himself sitting on a log beside it keeping warm. Before long Evie walked up and asked if she could sit with him. When he agreed she sat so close to him that she almost knocked him off of the log. As they talked one of he new men walked up to Scott and told him a few things that he did not know.

Come to find out the General had lied to Scott. The Mexican EMP guns were real. General Newton just was not sure if they headed east towards Palestine or north to Mexia. Knowing that Newton was heading to Palestine Scott decided that the Texican Militia would head north to Mexia.

When the sun came up Scott had all of the new men stand in formation. He needed to know their names and ranks that they had with Newton. With Julio not doing much Scott asked if he would like to be an adjutant. Scott told Julio that he needed

someone to take notes for him. Julio jumped at the opportunity.

Scott found that he had thirty six new Texicans; thirty one men and five women. Including Julio the Texican Militia now had forty eight men and eight women. Scott promoted Evie to the rank of Sergeant and put her over all of the women. With Scott's permission Evie made her friend Lea Corporal under her.

Chapter 4

Re-Supplied

After Scott talked with the new Texicans they started their walk to Donnie and then on to Mexia. By time they reached Donnie the Newton Militia had problems. One of the Mexican battalions had reached the town of Buffalo. General Newton thinking that his money made him great leader got him and most of his men killed. The Mexican battalion was in Centerville when they heard about General Newton's Militia being in Buffalo. In their goal of taking Texas hey moved north and came into Buffalo on Interstate 45. The fight only lasted one and a half hours.

Forty one members of Newton's Militia were captured and were being taken north to Teague. A few warehouses there were being used as POW camps for any Texas militia members that were captured.

Three days later the Texican Militia came within four miles of Mexia. There they found a company of Mexican troops. They had a few Humvees with one trailer attached to one of them. Something was on the trailer that Scott had never seen before. Knowing that his fifty seven man militia was no match for a one hundred twenty man company of trained Mexican soldiers Scott held back until it got dark.

As the Texicans waited in the shadows of trees and bushes Evie came to Scott and asked what he was going to do.

"I don't know yet." he said. "I need to pray about it."

Evie was starting to like Scott more than she knew but she also knew that sticking with him was the best thing that she could do. As Scott walked off to be alone while he prayed Evie sat there also praying.

"God ... he needs your help. I believe his story about you

taking him to he'll and then to heaven but ... now what do we do?"

Right at that moment she felt something; a voice in her heart. *He needs you Evie.* Evie stood and walked out to Scott. Standing in front of him she put her arms around him and lay her head on his chest. He wrapped his arms around her and they prayed together. Then they both heard a whisper that seemed to come from all around.

"*Unto you both I will give this land.*"

Scott and Evie both heard the same thing and knew that it was God giving them a promise. But what did God mean; "Unto you both?" They both liked each other but that was all. The word love never came to them. We they to stay together? There were so many questions and no answers.

That night Scott and Evie slept together holding each other but right in plane sight of the others so that no one would think that anything was going on. They were just staying warm in the cold night air.

The next morning one of rhe guards woke Scott up to a pot of coffer brewing over a campfire.

"I didn't want any fires." Scott angrily said to the guard as he kicked dirt on the fire. "We're to close to the Mexican camp."

Then a whistle blew down the road and gunfire opened up. The Texicans jumped up from where they were sleeping and opened fire on the flashes of light from the gun barrels down the road. It was still dark so no one could see anything. After a while the shooting stopped and the Mexican language could be heard down the road towards Mexia.

Suddenly Julio stood and yelled as loud as he could; "El Diablo." Then after a few Mexicans yelled orders to their soldiers it got quiet.

Two hours later it got daylight enough to see down the road towards Mexia. The Mexican soldiers had fled in the dark.

Scott looked at Julio and thanked him. "They are scared of you; El Diablo."

"I told you that I did not like being called the Devil.

"But Sir…" Julio sad. "They are not scared of you. They are scared of the Devil … El Diablo."

"I understand." Scott said as he lay his hand on Julio's shoulder. "But I still don't like it."

There was no doubt that the Mexicans knew that the Texicans were there. On the other hand they feared El Diablo and they knew that El Diablo was also there. Scott may have not liked being called The Devil but he decided to use it as a weapon if he could.

Knowing that an ambush could be set for them ahead the Texicans slowly worked their way into the southern side of Mexia. Once bedside the old National Guard Armory they stopped to rest. Scott could see at least half a mile in all four directions and nothing was moving.

"Which way do you think they went?" Scott asked Julio.

"Sorry Sir." Julio replied. "The Captain never even told the rest of us what we were doing."

"I know Mexia a little and I am thinking that they went to the east." Scott said. "The problem is that they could go left into the town itself or to the right to … I don't know where."

After a thirty minute rest Scott ordered the Texicans to fallow him to the east. He sent Evie and the other women to scout ahead.

"You sending her up there where an ambush could be waiting?" James asked."

"She has a job to do like the rest of us." Scott replied with no feelings at all.

The Texican Militia took the road to the east until it came to a "T". Then he had Evie turn to the left. Scott and the others fallowed them. When they came to Highway 84 Scott had everyone stop. There was still no hint as to where the Mexican soldiers had gone. With night coming Scott had the others scatter to the four corners of that crossroad to hide. There would be no fires that night.

As Scott hunkered down between two bushes Evie sat on the ground beside him. He held her and kept her warm. Storm clouds were moving in and they all knew that it was going to be a long night. About an hour later the bottom of the clouds dropped out and a heavy rain began to fall. Just seconds after the rain hit the temperature started dropping.

Scott pulled his camouflaged poncho over the two of them and they fell asleep. He had guards set out in four directions all night. No one was going to sneak up on them that night. One time during the night three Mexican soldiers walked up the middle of the main road. As long as none of he Texicans moved they should not be seen. The soldiers were more interested in telling jokes than looking around like they were suppose to have been doing.

The Mexican three man patrol walked down to around the old Walmart store and then came back. The heavy rain covered any sounds that any of the Texicans might have made and hiding in shadows of bushes and trees hid them. However; Scott was a believer in Murphy's Law. *If anything can go wrong it will.*

Movement to the soldier's left drew their attention. As they walked to the bushes they hoped to find a rabbit to cook up for breakfast. When they got close enough one of the female Texicans stood and opened fire killing all three of them.

"Move it." Scott ordered to all of the Texicans. He ran up towards the Walmart parking lot with his militia behind him. A few minutes later he looked far down the road and saw a platoon of Mexican soldiers searching the bushes around the dead soldiers. After a good thirty minutes a truck came down to them and picked up the dead soldiers. Then the soldiers fallowed the truck back to the main group farther up the road.

Scott called for Corporal Bishop. When he reported Scott promoted him to Sergeant and told him to take two men with him to scout out the Mexican's camp. Bishop took the other two black Texicans.

"We are told that white Americans hated the black Americans." Julio told Scott.

"Oh there are some that hate each other but to much anymore." Scott told Julio. "Bishop there is a country boy and he is good at this. He used to hunt wild hogs at night all the time."

Bishop took the other two blacks with him far down Highway 84 which ran all the way through Mexia. It was called by many the main drag. Suddenly gunfire opened up. They had walked into an ambush. One of Bishop's men was hit three times and died there on the ground.

Bishop and the other man ran to the side of a building where they took cover. Taking quick glances around the corner of he building Bishop saw at least twenty Mexican soldiers working their way towards him. Some of them were working their way around the back of the building. Seeing that they would be caught in crossfire seconds Bishop and the other man ran to the building next door and hid in the bushes. After a few minutes the Mexican soldiers started walking back to their main group.

When the Mexican soldiers were at least two hundred yards down the road Bishop yelled out; "El Diablo."

Fear filled the soldiers so quickly that even without looking back they all started running. Bishop and the other man went back to their dead friend. Taking turns they carried their friend back to where Scott and the others were. As they lay their friend at Scott's feet the others came around. Scott knelt beside the dead man.

"I would give you a medal if I had one." Scott said just barely loud enough for anyone to hear.

Scott stood and told the others that there was no place to bury the man and that they would have to leave him where he was. The man had an AR-15 so Scott asked if anyone wanted to trade rifles. One of the women came up with a Marlin .22 caliber rifle. He handed the AR-15 to her and took the Marlin. Then he smashed the Marlin against the asphalt parking lot so that no one else could use it against them.

"Alright!" Scott said. "Let's get ready to move."

Taking a street away from the main drag the Texicans went three blocks before turning back towards the Mexican soldiers. Scott warned the others that they were taking a flanking move to get to one side of the Mexicans and that they needed to move slow and quietly. The Mexican soldiers might be spread farther out that just three blocks.

Slowly Scott moved ahead stopping every few feet to look ahead for movement. The others were spread out sticking to the shadows of the buildings, trees, and bushes. After advancing eleven blocks Scott could hear the Mexican language being spoken. They were close. Scott raised his hand and spread his fingers open wide. This was to let the others know to spread out.

Scott send Lieutenant Bowers to the north to go up one block and move in when he did. The he promoted Sergeant Evie Deacon to Lieutenant and sent her and the women one block to the south. When both Lieutenants were in position Scott started moving towards the west where he Mexican soldiers were. Hopefully the EMP gun that he had seen earlier was there as well.

Five blocks up Scott stopped. Two Mexican soldiers were walking towards him checking things out. One was on one side of the street and the other one was on the other side. He pulled his knife. James saw that and pulled his knife as well. Just as the Mexican soldiers reached Scott and James they jumped out of the shadows and grabbed the soldiers. Three stabs in the back was enough to stop the soldier's struggling. With the Mexican soldiers dead the Texicans were still unseen. The Mexican soldiers ahead of them had no idea that they were coming.

Two more blocks ahead and Scott could see movement. It looked like the Mexican soldiers had a big campfire just five or six blacks ahead. Many of the soldiers could be seen walking around. They had no concern about the Texicans that had been seen.

Suddenly gunfire opened up to Scott's right. Lieutenant Bowers had started his attack before Scott was ready. Instantly Scott stood and started running towards the campfire. As soon as he was close enough he started firing. The others behind him opened fire as well. Scott was hoping to draw attention to him and Lieutenant Bowers so that Evie and the other women might be safer. However; that plan did not work.

Gunfire opened up to Scott's left and he knew that Evie's

group was under attack. No matter how much he liked her he knew that he could not leave to help her. He had his own job to do. After another minute of knowing that Evie could be killed he sent seven of his men to help her. This only left him with five men. It was a bad decision and he knew it but he also could not help himself.

As Scott and his group advanced he could hear the men he sent to help Evie opening fire on the enemy. As he approached the enemy's camp fire he and his men shot the last of the Mexicans in that area. Then he heard the shooting from Evie's area stop. Scott turned to his right to help Lieutenant Bowers. By time his group got there the Lieutenant had already done his job.

The Texicans met up back at the Mexican campfire. Three Mexican soldier had been wounded and captured. Two others were captured without wounds. Scott had four of the Mexican soldiers shot on the spot. Then he had the one survivor brought to him.

With Julio translating he told the soldier; "I am El Diablo." the soldier fell to his knees in fear. "I'm setting you free. You will go find other Mexicans and tell them that El Diablo is coming for them as well. I am taking the souls of these dead men around you to Hell where they belong." Scott took two steps toward the crying soldier. "You tell your commanders that I have a specially hot place for them. You all have one of two choices. You can go home and leave Texas alone or … I can take all your souls back to Hell."

Scott turned and walked away after giving orders to release the soldier but, unarmed. As the soldier started to walk away someone fired and hit the soldier dropping him to the ground. Scott looked to his left and saw Private Mickey yelling.

"You're stupid. We shouldn't be letting any of the enemy free."

Scott quickly raised his rifle and pointed it at Mickey. "Drop your weapon."

Mickey stared at Scott and then slowly turned his rifle towards Scott but three of the other Texicans took him to the ground and disarmed him. Then the three men stood Mickey up to face Scott.

"I am tired of you disobeying my orders. This time you may have ruined my plans just because you did not know what I was doing. Well let me tell you. I needed this man to go back to the others and tell them what El Diablo had done here. That name will do more damage to their moral than all of our weapons together. I do not have to explain everything I do to you."

Scott asked Evie and her women to stand in line for a firing squad. Mickey was stood in front of them and held in place by two other Texicans. Right in front of the Mexican soldier Scott gave to order to fire. A split second later Mickey fell dead.

"Now listen." Scott yelled out. "We are a militia. Allof you may come and go as you wish but ... as long as you are fighting with us you will fallow orders. If you do not like an order then leave but ... if you openly disobey an order I will have you shot." Scott looked around. "Do you understand me?"

All of the Texicans agreed to fallow Scott and fallow his orders. The soldier had only been shot in the arm. After his wounds were attended to and he was fed and given water Scott had Julio give him one more message. "El Diablo can also be also merciful ... at times." Then the Mexican soldier was released with extra food and two canteens of water.

When the soldier left he was heading off to the south. Scott hoped that the soldier would know where the other Mexicans might be. He ordered the others to set up camp with only the one campfire the Mexicans had. He then had the Texicans spread out to hide in the bushes and shadows in case more Mexicans came. The fire could be used for a while to cook anything they needed cooked. Many of the dead Mexican soldiers had smoked pork and dried rice on them.

Seven of the Texicans had been killed with only one wounded. There were only forty eight Texicans now. Scott rested in the shadows and thought about this. After a while Evie found him and sat beside him. He held her in his arms where she fell asleep.

"Father."* Scott whispered to himself. *"I need more soldiers. I cannot do this with just the few I have. I know that the only way we won this fight was because you were with us."

Then a soft voice filled the air around him. *"I am the same yesterday, today, and tomorrow."*

"What is that suppose to mean Lord?"

The voice cam back saying. *"I was with you yesterday and today. Why should I not be with you tomorrow?"*

"I still need more soldier."

God did not say anything else to Scott that night but he knew that God was and always will be with him.

At that time one of he night guards walked up to Scott. "I have something to show you Sir."

Scott fallowed the guard to a trailer. On if was one of the EMP guns. For a while he just stood there and looked at it. "Bring both of my Lieutenants to me." he ordered the guard.

A few minutes later Evie and Bowers showed up and stood beside him. He ordered them to find some explosives to blow up the ENP gun. The Mexican soldiers and their gear were searched but only seven pounds of C-4 were found.

"That will be enough." Scott said a she set the explosives at different places on the EMP gun.

After attaching deck cord to the explosives by wrapping each stick of C-4 three times with the cord he attached the other end to a black fuse. Then he lit the black fuse which burned slowly giving everyone time to get away. When the black fuse hit the deck cord the entire gun exploded. Deck cord burns at 23,000 feet per second and, although it is a fuse it set all of the C-4 off at one time. The EMP gun was totally destroyed.

The explosion was so loud that it drew attention of an entire Mexican Battalion in Waco. Until they heard the explosion they were to head north the next morning. The Commanding officer of that Battalion changed his mind. He knew that at least one of he EMP guns was in that direction and decided to go protect it.

Brigade General Sanchez got his men ready and within an hour they were on their way east.

The rest of the night went by quietly for the Texicans. They finally got the rest they deserved. What they did not know was that eight hundred Mexicans; an entire brigade was heading their way. With nothing between them and the Texican Militia to stop them they moved quickly.

Brigade general Sanchez moved his brigade through Mart and Groesbeck destroying everything in their path. The two towns were decimated. With over half of their building burned and population killed there was not much left. By time he and his brigade reached Mexia Scott and the Texicans had made their way north to Fairfield.

Scott decided to work his way to Dallas where General Bolton said that he could be rearmed by Central Command. He did not like his militia to be controlled by anyone else but the weapons that his Texicans had were not going to work well against the Mexicans. He had no choice. Their AR-15s and .22 caliber rifles were okay against smaller groups, larger groups at battalion size were on their way. He also hoped to grow in numbers on their way.

Brigade General Sanchez was furious when he found the EMP gun destroyed. There were only five left, two still in Waco and three in Houston under another Brigade commander. He started questioning the civilians and anyone that did not know anything was executed.

The General had become even more savage that he already was. One old man did give Sanchez a piece of information that he could use. Those that blew up the EMP gun left town and headed north. The day before leaving Mexia a young soldier came into Sanchez's camp and told him about the leader of the group he was after. When he mentioned the name El Diablo fear filled the hearts of everyone there. They had already heard of El Diablo and his ability to destroy any Mexican in his way.

Now Brigade General Sanchez knew that this El Diablo was only a man that lead a small group of people. El Diablo may have been a savage leader but he still only had a small group. He had crushed other small groups of men and women and he would crush this El Diablo and his group as well.

By time Brigade General Sanchez left Mexia only ten percent of the population of that town still existed. His new goal was to crush this new threat that put fear in all of his soldiers. Once he crushed this El Diablo he would be feared by the remaining Texicans. With luck he would be the next governor of the state of Texas, Mexico.

Before leaving Fairfield he had another thirty three men and women join the Texicans. This gave him sixty nine men and twelve women. Before leaving he gave them the usual speech.

"We are a militia. You may come and go as you wish but, while you are with me you will fallow orders or I will order your being shot."

Scott made one of the men from Fairfield Lieutenant and put him in charge of he thirty men that joined. Lieutenant Mitch Davisson had been a Lieutenant in the army and had seen action in Afghanistan. He was a thirty two year old black man that quickly earned Scott's respect. Although Scott and Davisson did not know each other in Afghanistan they both had served under General Bolton there.

By time the Texicans reached Dallas they had picked up another sixty four more people. This made the Texican Militia one hundred forty five strong. The Texicans finally found Central Command where Scott also found General Bolton. Bolton and his militia were also there for supplies.

"How many do you have now?" Bolton asked Scott.

"One hundred forty five including me." Scott proudly confessed.

"You know ..." Bolton said. "... there's a large group here that are about to head south to look for you. They want to join you too."

"I don't know if I can command that many people." Scott said.

"It is just like commanding the ones you have now." Bolton

advised. "You can do it Captain. Oh by the way... I think Command will be wanting to raise your rank."

"Why?"

"You almost commanding a battalion now. You should be a least a Major."

"What ever." Scott said with a laugh. "I thought you wanted me to be president."

"Maybe later." Bolton said also laughing.

Bolton led the Texicans to Central Command where the Texican Militia went through a complete refitting. Every Texican was given an M-16 of their own and other gear like web belts, canteens, and daggers. They were also given camouflaged clothing, boots and three pares of socks and backpacks to carry things in.

Scott was taken to where he was given a humvee of his own and two personnel carriers. The others would have to walk. Two large trucks were also given to him for carrying supplies. By the end of he day the Texicans were fully fitted enough to fight a sizable force.

That evening Bolton took Scott to see Central Command itself. Three en sat in large chairs behind a long desk. The one in the middle informed Scott that his militia had been outfitted and he was to obey orders from them from then on. Scott did not like this but if his militia was to be better armed than they were then he had to agree.

First they gave him the rank of Major. While the Texas National Guard was on the northern border of the Republic of Texas many of the militias were on the southern border. However; they wanted the Texas Militia to go back to central Texas wipe out the Mexican forces there. At least they would be close to their homes.

By time Central Command was finished with Scott it was dark. Bolton took him back out to where his militia and supplies was waiting. Bolton wished him well and left. Evie and many of the others gathered around Scott as he told them what had happened. He was told that there were many that wanted to see him about joining the Texican Militia but he said he would see them in the morning. He was tired.

Scott woke up only one time during the night and found Evie fast asleep in his arms. After wrapping his arm around her he fell asleep too. It was a long night but they all got more sleep they needed so badly.

Scott woke up the next morning to someone making coffee over the campfire. He saw Evie sitting in a folding chair drinking a cup of he brew so he got up and joined her. By time the sun came up Evie had moved beside her man and had her arm around him. They talked for a while at first and then he got quiet. When she asked him what was bothering him he told her what all happened in Central Command.

As the sun came up more and more Scott saw people standing around him. These were the ones wanting to join the Texicans. They had heard about El Diablo and of all of the destruction the Texican Militia had done. They wanted to be a part of it.

Scott stood and looked them over. "My God. How many are there?"

"Closed to one thousand and they only want to join you." Evie said.

Scott called for Lieutenants Bowers and Davisson. When they got there he instructed all thereof them to get their people in line and the new people in a separate line. There was a lot of yelling and in thirty minutes he had them all in lines for inspection.

First he promoted his Lieutenants to Captains. They were to split the new members up into companies and make one of them a Lieutenant for each company. He even promoted James to Captain and had him choose twenty people that could help him in any scavenging. After his usual peach he asked how many had joined. It seemed that the Texican Militia now had just over five hundred members. The Texican Militia had grown to just under a battalion size.

When everyone was ready to go Scott climbed into his

humvee and lead the others out. His three Lieutenants also rode with him leaving their lieutenants in charge of the Texicans under them.

Chapter 5

The Threat Within

Scott could not believe how much Central Command had given them. Not knowing that a battalion of Mexican soldier was working their way north Scott was taking the Texican Militia south.

Four days later the Texicans found themselves walking into the town of Fairfield. The entire western side of the town had been destroyed. As the Texicans walked into town those that lived there came to them. They told Scott how that the Mexican soldiers came in from the south and just started killing everyone and destroying every building they could see. Finally a man walked up to Scott and said that he was the unofficial mayor of the town.

Scott sat down with Mayor Duval in what used to be a large restaurant. There the two talked for over three hours. Duval offered free food and water if the Texicans stayed the night; a few days if they could. Scott agreed. It was going to be a cold night so the Texicans would spend the night in the restaurant itself.

All evening and into the night the people of Fairfield brought food to the Texicans. Food that would last a while was stored in one of the trucks. Food that had to be eaten quickly was eaten.

That night many of the people came to Scott to tell him things they saw and heard. Many of the young women had been kidnapped by the Mexican soldiers and anyone that resisted was simply shot. This was also the first that Scott heard about the group of Mexican soldiers being at battalion size. When the Mexican soldiers left they headed west. The Texicans missed them by only one day.

The next morning Scott woke up to Evie making more coffee. It was still another hour of two before daylight but he got up anyway. He wanted to go after Brigade General Sanchez but his one hundred forty five soldiers would be no match for the almost eight hundred Mexican soldiers. Although Sanchez was a Brigade General in rank he really only commanded a battalion.

As the sun came up more and more people of Fairfield came to Scott about joining his militia. More were coming in from surrounding towns. The word was getting out that El Diablo was in Fairfield. Scott only hoped that the Sanchez had not heard that he was there.

As more and more people came in Scott saw that they could not leave. Sanchez would just have to get away this time. But, they could not wait to long. They would leave the next morning.

By that night over three hundred more people had joined; Scot's militia, as many called them. Scott did not get much sleep that night while more people continued to come in to join the Texican Militia.

Around midnight Scott stepped out into a nearby field for some privacy.

"I need a lot more fighters Father. I still cannot fight this Sanchez and his battalion of seasoned fighters with only the four hundred or so fighters I have."

The words started running through his mind; *"They are coming."*

By the next morning the Texican Militia gained another one hundred twenty people. Scott had the Texicans get their gear together and loaded into the trucks. Around 1000 hours they finally left Fairfield. Taking Highway 84 towards Mexia Scott wanted to find Sanchez's Battalion of Mexican soldiers but he also hoped he would not find them. Sanchez had the Texicans outnumbered almost two to one and the Mexican soldiers were experienced fighters. All of the Texicans, except for Julio were civilians with rifles.

Sanchez knew that he and El Diablo were running all over central Texas trying to find each other so he set up defenses in

Mexia. Then he sent a man to Fairfield to tell Scott that he was waiting. However; he had no idea that the Texican Militia had grown in numbers. His last report was that the Texicans were only about fifty strong.

Three days later the Texican Militia was walking into the town of Teague. As they walked through the town on Highway 84 Scott saw a Mexican soldier walking towards him carrying a white flag.

"Hold your fire." Scott ordered the others as he halted their advance.

Scott sent three men out to get the Mexican soldier and bring him back. The three men took the soldier's flag from him and patted him down for any weapons. Then they brought him to Scott.

"Do you speak English?" Scott asked the soldier.

"Yes." the soldier said. "This is why the great Senior Brigade General Sanchez sent me."

Scott stepped back a step and looked at Julio. "The great?" he commented. "Why not the great and powerful?" Julio and many around him laughed.

"I'm El Diablo … the great and powerful El Diablo." Scott said with a big smile on his face.

The soldier fell to his knees and begged El Diablo not to take his soul to Hell.

"I'll spare your soul under one condition." Scott said. Then he grabbed the soldier by the shirt sleeve and added; "You will take a message back to Senior wetback Sanchez."

"Yes … anything." the quivering soldier agreed.

"You will give this message to that wetback." Scott said. "I am on my way."

The soldier stopped quivering and asked; "That's all."

"Yes … that is all." Scott said. "Tell him that I am on my way."

The Mexican soldier was given food and water but his rifle and pistol was not given back to him. Then he was sent on his way. Scott watched the soldier leave Teague on his way to Mexia and his lord and master Sanchez. Then he looked up into the sky and prayed.

"Okay Lord. It's in your hands now."
Then the words came to Scott; *"Wait two days."*

Scott ordered the Texicans to set up camp on the west side of Teague; just west of the railroad overpass over Highway 84. Then he sent out one platoon of Texicans about one mile west of the main camp to watch for any advances of Mexican troops. Lieutenant Garver commanding the 1st Platoon under Captain Bowers' "A" Team volunteered for this mission.

"What are you doing?" a Sergeant asked Scott. "We should be moving ahead and attacking those Mexicans."

"And just who are you?" Scott asked with other officers around the campfire laughing at the young man.

The man stood tall and answered; "I am Sergeant Rogers of 3rd. Platoon; C Company ... Sir."

"Well Sergeant ..." Scott said trying to word his response properly. "... why do you think we should do that?"

The Sergeant seemed to loose control as he explained. "We're just sitting ducks sitting here like fools. We should be attacking them before they attack us."

"You're forgetting your place Sergeant." Captain Davisson said as he stood. "You come to me before you come to the Major."

"But Sir ..." the Sergeant said before being stopped by his Captain.

"But nothing Sergeant ... or do you want me to start calling you ... Corporal?" Captain Davisson said with a very angry tone in his voice. "I'll be back at our camp later. Then you can talk to me about any disagreements you have with command. Understand ... Sergeant?"

"Yes Sir." Sergeant Rogers said as he turned and walked away.

"I'm sorry Sir." Captain Davisson said to Scott. He reminds

me a lot of Private Mickey … the man you had shot in Mexia."

"Oh!" Scott said. "So this Sergeant thinks he knows everything too."

"He is a smart man and a good soldier but he does have that one problem. I argue with him all the time." Captain Davisson said.

"Then maybe you and his Platoon Lieutenant should have a talk with him." Scott advised. "I have no problem with lower ranks giving their ideas on things but I am a stickler with using the chain of command. If this man cannot use the chain of command then maybe he would serve us better as a Corporal of even Private."

"His Lieutenant and I will talk with him one last time Sir." Captain Davisson advised.

"Good enough." Scott agreed.

It had been dark for over an hour when Scott decided to turn in. He got up and told the others there that he would see them in the morning. Then he went to his tent which four of the Texicans had set up earlier. As he looked at the bed he saw Evie laying on it.

"I know." she said. "You have to write in your journal for awhile before going to bed."

"No!" Scott said with a smile. "I was wondering why you are in my bed."

"Well … I can leave if you want." Evie said.

Scott thought for a moment and then said; "You don't have to leave but, what are your intentions?"

"If you don't know my intentions by now then you're in trouble." Eve said with a smile. "Besides! I thought that you have been wanting me to sleep with you."

"I have but this creates a problem." Scott advised. "I cannot show you any favors. Others will be expecting this."

"I don't expect any favors Scott…or may I call you that?"

"It's okay when we are alone but out there it is still Major." Scott advised her.

"No problem … Scott." Evie said with a sexy smile. "Now

finish your journal and get in bed."

It's not going to be easy to write in my journal tonight. Scott thought to himself. When he finished his writing Scott went to bed. For many hours he and Evie just held each other and talked. Finally they both fell asleep still holding each other. There was no sex that night; just the pleasure of holding each other.

That night a camp guard woke up Scott and Evie with a report of three Mexican soldiers being captured. Lieutenant Garver's Platoon had a short gunfight with a small group of Mexican soldiers and these three were captured. All of the others but one were killed. The one escaped and retreated back to the others in Mexia.

Scott and Evie got dressed and walked outside to the three soldiers. Using Julio as a translator he asked them questions after letting them know that he was El Diablo. With them sufficiently scared almost to death he asked his questions.

Come to find out these soldiers had left their camp in Mexia without permission. They wanted to become famous for being the ones that killed El Diablo.

"I never thought that they would do that. " Scott said. "This Sanchez could send a group just to kill me."

Then he looked at Captain James and ordered him to double the camp guards from then on. James' scavengers had become more camp guards at night than scavengers. They were mostly older men and were better suited for this than fighting battles. In battles they were the ones that stayed back and guarded the two trucks and supplies.

Scott's questioning continued. Through Julio Scott learned that Sanchez's Battalion was only about six hundred strong. Over two hundred had deserted over the past month out of fear of fighting El Diablo. When they were sent out to find the Texican Militia Sanchez was loosing about twenty to thirty a night. The desertions were so bad that any Mexican soldier caught walking past the outer guards were shot on sight. This was good news to Scott.

All of the information that Scott got from the prisoners

came from only one of them. The other two would not talk. When Scott had finished questioning the prisoners he had the two that refused to talk shot. He then released the other one to go back and tell the other Mexicans in Mexia that El Diablo killed the other two but showed mercy to him.

Scott knew that the Mexican soldier would tell his superiors that he lied to El Diablo but that did not matter. He would also tell them that El Diablo killed the two that refused to cooperate. The soldier was given food and water and then sent on his way.

A young Sergeant walked up and yelled out for all to hear. “Some kind of leader you are.” It was Sergeant Rogers again. “You should kill any prisoners we catch … all of them not just two of three.”

“Hold your tongue.” Scott yelled at Rogers.

“You don’t know what you’re doing.” Rogers yelled again.

“The Major told you to hold your tongue.” a Lieutenant told Rogers. Then he turned to Scott and added; “I’m sorry Sir. Captain Davisson and I talked with this man but he refuses to listen to us.”

“You’re his Lieutenant?” Scott asked.

“Yes Sir.” the young man snapped. I am Lieutenant Parker of Company C, 3rd Platoon.”

“Lieutenant.” Scott said. “Please take this man back to your Captain and do what ever you want but; do something.”

“Yes Sir.” the Lieutenant said. Then he turned his attention to the Sergeant and yelled; “Let’s go Corporal.”

“I’m a Sergeant.” Rogers yelled.

“Not after we talk with the Captain.”

The Lieutenant and Sergeant walked away with Rogers still yelling about Scott being a bad leader. He was even insisting that he should be leading this militia. Scott looked at some of those around him and started laughing.

“Anyone want that dumb ass running this militia?” Scott asked.

Those around him started laughing as well. What Scott and many of he others around him did not know was that Rogers had many supporters that just stayed quiet. A small rebellion against Scott was forming and no one knew it.

Later that evening Captain Davisson and Lieutenant Parker walked up to Scott who was sitting at a campfire. They told him that Parker had been reduced to the rank of Corporal and he was told that if he wanted to be a Private again all he had to do was continue mouthing off.

"Thank you Captain ... Lieutenant." Scott said. "I don't Mindanao the Texicans telling me how they feel about things but there are proper ways of doing it."

"Like using the chain of command." Lieutenant Parker said.

Scott and a few others sat around the campfire for a few more hours before Scott got up and went to his tent. As soon as he stepped in the tent he saw Evie laying in bed.

"You've had a hard day with Rogers and all." Evie said.

"I'll be okay." Scott said as he sat down to write in his journal.

There was a great deal more to write about than the previous night so he was at his folding desk a while longer. He had to write about the three prisoners and what was done with them and why. Then he had to write about Rogers. He ended his notes on Rogers with the comment; "I expect more trouble from him."

When Scott crawled into bed he and Evie held each other again. As with the night before they talked for a long time while holding each other. Also as with the first night of them sleeping together; on this second night there was no sex. Both fell asleep just holding each other.

The next morning everyone was awaken around 0300 hours to break camp and get ready to move out. Again Rogers expressed his feelings by saying that it was about time that the Texicans did something. This time his followers showed themselves. Out of the five hundred sixty five Texicans Rogers had over one hundred on his side. Just one day out of Teague Scott had Rogers arrested and brought before him

Scott had, had enough of Rogers and stopped the Texicans advance to Mexia around noon. He could not continue as long as he had so many rebelling against him. As Scott sat in a chair behind a folding table Rogers was brought to him with his hands tied behind his back.

"You have been charged with inciting a rebellion against me and the Texican Militia." Scott said but Rogers was unable to shut up.

"I am only guilty of telling everyone that you area bad leader and we need to choose another leader." Rogers yelled.

After Rogers was gagged Scott continued. "We have already executed one man that tried to take over and; if you are found guilty then you will be facing the possibility of also being executed."

Scott went on to build the case against Rogers and then Rogers was given the chance to defend himself. The gag was removed from his mouth and he was untied. He called many of those that fallowed him and gave one example after another for why Scott should not be the leader of the Texicans and why he should be. He got many laughs from those that did not fallow him. He even told everyone that Scott really believed that he was the real El Diablo.

After almost two hours of talking Scott had him shut up and sit down. Then he started defending the offenses against him.

"I do not believe that I and really El Diablo but using that against the Mexicans is part of my strategy. Many of the things that Rogers said is true but you all know why I did those things. Over and over I have lead this militia through tough times. We will loose people in every conflict. That cannot be helped. But Rogers has tried to change this trial into me defending myself. He is the one being charged and he alone is on trial. We are a militia. That means that every one of you come and go as you wish but; while you are here you will fallow my orders or I will have you shot."

Scott sat down just as a bullet whizzed by his head. Brigade General Sanchez had send half of his Battalion to attack the Texicans. As everyone scrambled to hide behind trees Rogers was forgotten about. As it got darker the battle continued. Many of the smaller skirmishes were close ones with the distance between the two sides only being a few feet. There were even many knife fights.

The fighting went on through the night. Around 0200 hours Scott was shot in the right side of his chest. He was down and Captain Davisson took command. Evie wanted to take care of Scott but she had her own company to command. Captain James having nothing much to do took care of Scott. He had his men protect the Major at all cost. By 0400 hours the shooting almost completely stopped.

When the shooting did finally stop Evie went back to Scott. By this time the bullet had been removed and he was patched up. When the sun came up the other Captains came and gave Scott their report.

About three hundred of the Mexicans that attacked them had been killed. About ten others had escaped. Two hundred ten of the Texicans had been killed. The problem was that almost all of them were Texicans that did not fallow Rogers. It did not take long for Rogers to walk into the tent where Scott was saying that he was taking over. Then he went outside where his followers were holding the others that fallowed Scott.

"Those of you that want to follow me may do so but you will fallow my orders. The rest of you can stay here with false leader of yours. He is in this tent dying."

Then he had those that chose to stay disarmed. He had his own men take control of the humvee and two trucks full of supplies. When Rogers left with his men those that stayed behind with Scott were counted. Two hundred ninety men went with Rogers leaving two hundred seventy five behind with Scott.

Two hours after Rogers and his group left Scott and the others Scott woke up. He missed Rogers' coming into the tent to say that he had taken over. Scott was waking slow but Evie was there holding his hand. Evie told him what all happened and informed him how many stayed with him.

"Less than half." Scott whispered. "How many of my officers stayed with me?"

"All of them." Evie told him. Mostly lower ranks went with Rogers.

"Have everyone leave the tent except you." Scott insisted.

Once everyone left Evie held onto his hand as he prayed.

***"Father? I have done what you told me to do. I was brutal when I had to be but showed mercy at other times. Why have you allowed this to happen to me? Now I cannot be nice when I find Rogers. I cannot show him any mercy."* Scott took a few breaths and then continued. *"What do you want me to do? This war will continue with or without me. What do you want from me? Why do you not listen to me?"* Scott said as tears flooded his eyes.**

Then God spoke through Evie saying; *"I promised to be with you at all times. Why do you not listen to me?"*

Evie used her shirt and wiped Scott's tears from his face. Then in a solid voice he told Evie to set him up on the side of the bed. Then he asked her to call in his Captains. When they came in he told them to help him outside.

"They have got to see me still alive and doing well." Scott told his Captains.

With the help of his Captains Scott stepped outside his tent. As everyone cheered he stood tall and looked around. Then he spoke to them.

"I feel like kicking some … butts." The crowd yelled in support again. "We will rest two more days before we leave."

"Where are we going?" someone from the crowd yelled.

"Mexia."

"But Rogers took all of our rifles and pistols." the same man said.

"God will supply us with what we need."

"I'm not a Christian." the same man said. "I do not believe in God but I do believe in you."

Scott thought for a moment and then said; "If God has not supplied you with the means to defeat Sanchez and his men by time we get to Mexia then we will turn back."

The man and many of the others were happy with that. They all stayed with Scott because he had never lead them wrong. Scott used the next two days to rest. The medics he had said that he was healing faster than he should and everyone knew why. Around 0300 hours of the third day Scott stood in the middle of the camp and ordered everyone to break camp. Then he ordered James to stay behind with his men to watch over all of he gear until he came back with the trucks.

Then Scott walked out of the camp with the others behind him. Mexia was a good two day march if everyone was in good shape. Because of the wounded insisting on coming along, including Scott himself, the trip would take four days. They took their time but they were persistent. Who ever they came to first; Rogers or Sanchez, the Texicans were going to wipe them out.

Chapter 6

The Trials

As the Texicans got closer two of James' men which had been scouting ahead came back to Scott with news. They were still four miles from Mexia but Rogers and his group were just ahead. The two men took Scott to where they spotted Rogers and his group. As Scott looked over the area he saw the two trucks sitting in a field with no guards around them. *Stupid idiot.* he thought about Rogers. Then he sent two of James' men to get the trucks.

As the two men worked their way to the two trucks Scott wondered why Rogers had not yet attacked the Mexicans. Suddenly the trucks motors started and the drivers drove them out of the field. One of the trucks stopped when the driver got shot but the other one continued. Luckily it was the truck that had all of the Texicans weapons in it.

Rogers group continued to fire as the truck drove past Scott and stopped. Scott ordered the driver to take the truck to the others almost a mile back. Scott and the others jumped on the truck as it continued on to the others. Within an hour of the truck arriving all of the Texicans were rearmed with the weapons that they had before Rogers took them. There were also many crates of MREs in the truck which was badly needed.

Scott set out guards and then allowed the Texicans to eat. By time it was getting dark all of the Texicans were fed and were ready to fight. Scott lead the Texicans back to where the trucks had been. This time the other truck was in the middle of Rogers' camp where it could be watched. Scott looked around and smiled.

Scott noticed that Rogers had set up his camp in a field of dried grass. After asking God for some help he felt a breeze on the back of his neck. The wind always blew out of the southwest but that night it blew out of the east. This was something that never happened. Scott spread out about forty men with matches. Then on his command they set the grass on fire.

As the forty men ran back to the other Texicans the night sky lit up. The wind picked up and the wall of flames caught half of Rogers' men sleeping. The others ran towards the waiting Mexicans. Screams filled the air as men and women in Rogers' group burned alive. Scott looked on as men and women that used to be his Texicans ran out of the flames as walking torches. Once he had to turn his head.

Those that escaped the flames ran towards the west and into the hands of the waiting Mexicans. They were cut down by rifles fire before they got very far from their burning friends. Those that fallowed Rogers did not stand a chance. Within an hour of the grass being set on fire Rogers and all of his men were dead either from the fire or being shot by the Sanchez and his soldiers.

Scott lead the Texicans through the burned grass and found the other truck and Humvee had been parked on a patch of gravel with no grass. They had been saved from the fire. When Scott came to Rogers' body he spat on him. The Texicans cheered when they saw that what Scott had promised came true. Even the Atheist had to admit that something strange had happened although they still would not admit that God had anything to do with it.

Some of the Texicans had their families with them including some of those that chose to go with Rogers. Scott feared that he children met the same fate that their parents found but, when he looked in the back of the second truck he found all of the children had been placed in it. *Thank you for saving the children Father.* Scott thought to himself.

The truck was driven one mile back from the field to get the children away from any attack from the Mexicans that might come. Then the children were tended to first. As the night went on the children were fed and given water. Then they were cleaned up and laid on blankets in the grass. Other blankets kept them warm that night. Scott had James and his men guard the children that night to keep any of them from venturing out to find their parents.

The next morning after the children had been fed Scott told them all what had happened to their parents. He did not lie to them and told them what happened. A few of the older children were angry at Scott for ordering the grass to be set on fire. In their eyes he killed heir parents and they did not care that their parents betrayed Scott and the other Texicans.

There were twelve children and seven of them wanted to go back to Teague. The youngest that wanted to leave was just fifteen years old. The two oldest were eighteen years old. Scott agreed to allow them to go back to Teague with three armed men taking them. He did not want these angry children having any weapons.

Three of James' men volunteered to take all twelve of the children back to the people of Teague. The three men and the children left at about noon that day. With them gone Scott turned his attention to Brigade General Sanchez and his soldiers.

Scott was led to the hill just before entering Mexia. He knew that the old Walmart store was to the left but he could not see it through the trees. He sent a fire team to check it out and see if it was being used by Sanchez. They returned an hour later with news that the Mexicans had moved all of the shelves outside and were using the building as a large barracks. Then they told him something that he did not want to hear. All of Sanchez's trucks were in the parking lot but there were no EMP guns. If Sanchez did not have the last two EMP guns then who did?

Fog was moving in and Scott got an idea. He had one of he trucks drive out into a field just northeast of Highway 84. The driver was not to use the headlights and he was to face the truck towards the southwest. The Mexicans were not to know that the truck was there. As the fog got thicker Scott walked out into the field a few feet from the truck. Then he fired three shots into the air and had the driver to turn on the truck's headlights.

All of the Mexicans started firing at Scott's shadow in the fog. Hundreds of rounds were fired while he just stood there. With the truck at the angle it was it looked like Scott was standing in the middle of Highway 84. As the Mexican soldiers fired at his shadow they were really firing about one hundred yards to Scott's left.

When the Mexicans finally stopped firing Scott yelled; "I am El Diablo and have come for all of your souls." Then he lowered himself to the ground making it look like he had melted into the ground itself. The driver turned the headlights off.

All of Sanchez's soldiers panicked and started running away. Some even opened fire on each other for some reason. In minutes Mexia was full of Mexican soldiers running out of the area and off to the north and west. Most of them dropped their rifles so that they could run faster. By time Sanchez gained control he only had just over one hundred soldiers left. The once Brigade General was now nothing more than a Company Commander whose soldiers were peeing in their pants.

Scott had the driver turn the headlights back on. Again the soldiers fired at the shadow. When they stopped Scott raised his rifle and yelled as loud as he could. Then he lowered his rifle and fired. Because of he fog Scott could not see any of the Mexican soldiers but he knew about where hey were. Luckily his shot hit one of the soldiers. As that soldier fell the others realized that they could not hurt El Diablo but El Diablo could kill them. Sanchez lost control again as his remaining men ran off to the north and west.

Scott ordered his Texicans to move in but try not to kill Sanchez. A few minutes later he was called on his radio. The area was cleared and Sanchez had been captured.

Scott and his Captains walked down the hill and into the Walmart parking lot. There he found Brigade General Sanchez on his knees. He looked down at the once great General and saw a well dressed man. His uniform had so many medals on it that pulled his coat down on the left side. At that timed about thirty Mexican soldiers that had been captured were brought in front of Scott. They were forced to their knees shaking and some even crying.

Scott looked at Captain Bowers and ordered him to remove

the General's medals. Bowers grabbed one medal at a time and ripped them off of Sanchez's uniform coat. With each medal being pulled off the coat tore. By time Bowers finished the General's uniform coat was a rag. Scott stepped back and pulled his pistol.

"I am El Diablo and I am taking your soul to Hell." Then he pointed his pistol at the head of Sanchez and fired. Then he gave the order; "Line these men up for execution." The Mexican soldiers were moved in a line. On their knees they were shot by other Texicans who enjoyed doing their duty. "I am El Diablo and I am taking your souls." Scott yelled as the soldiers were shot.

When three Mexican soldiers were left Scott stopped he executions. The soldiers were crying. With help from Julio translating his words Scott said; "I am El Diablo and I give your lives back to you." One of the three soldier almost passed out. "Go and tell your countrymen to leave the Republic of Texas or I'll take more of your souls."

The three soldiers were fed and given water. Then they were sent on their way. Again Scott noticed that they headed off to the south. Every time he released prisoners they ran towards he south. Were they running back to Mexico or did they know something that Scott did not know? Was there another battalion farther off to the south?

The Texicans cleared the Walmart store and parking lot of any dead Mexicans. Then Scott went through the trucks that were in the parking lot. Three of the trucks were full-face of Mexican MREs. What the Mexican army called MREs were nothing but the green cans that US troops used many years earlier. They may have been heavy and bulky but they were food.

Another truck had two crates of M-16s and twenty three crates of .223 ammunition that the American president had given them. The three World War Two jeeps were given to Scott's Captains although Evie would ride with him in his Humvee.

Scott ordered the Texicans to spend the next three days resting. Guards were sent out to protect those resting. Captain

Bowers was responsible for guarding Highway 84 east of Mexia. Captain Davisson had the areas north of Mexia and Evie had central and west Mexia. As usual James took care of the area around Walmart.

The Texicans were down to only two hundred ten fighters. However; as they rested in Mexia more people came in wanting to join the Texicans. Entire small militias were wanting to join. By time the third night had come Scott had about four hundred forty Texicans.

Scott wanted to see why all of the Mexican soldiers that he released headed south; on the morning of the fourth day he had the Texicans break camp to head south. During the night another thirty men and women joined the Texicans giving Scott four hundred seventy soldiers.

While the Texicans worked their way south on Highway 39 the older children that were being taken to Teague attacked the three men guarding them and killed them. After taking their rifles six of the oldest decided to return to Mexia to find and kill Scott for killing their parents. The oldest of the children was Robert Mia. He took command of the other five as they looked for Scott. The other children continued to Teague.

By time Mia's group of children reached Mexia the Texicans had been gone for two day. The youngest person in Mia's group was seventeen years old. Only three of them were armed with the rifles they took off of the three men that were taking them to Teague. Not knowing which direction the Texicans went Mia took his group to the south.

Not knowing that Mia and his group was behind them Scott had the Texicans stop just outside of the town of Jewett. Allowing the older Texicans to rest a few days Scott went into town for information. When the people of the town realized that Scott was the leader of the Texican Militia they came out and showered them with food and other things. With it getting colder some of he Texicans needed coats and jackets. Many of these items were also given to the Texicans.

One night gunfire was heard down Highway 39 towards

Mexia. Captain Davisson had some of his men watching the rear until the Texicans moved on. Seeing other Americans walking towards them the fire team thought nothing of Mia and his group walking up to them. By time they realized what was going on Mia's group had killed all but one of the fire team. That one man escaped and got word back to Scott. Those with Mia that had no weapons took them off of the dead Texicans.

As the man reported to Scott about what happened he had to admit that he did not know who they were that attacked them; only that they were white Americans. Scott quickly sent a platoon of Texicans from Davisson's Company "C". As the platoon got closer to Mia's Militia Mia had the others hide in the trees along the side of he highway. When the platoon passed Mia rook his Militia on to Scott's main camp.

Scott was still not at one hundred percent after being shot in Mexia. He was doing better than anyone expected him to be doing but he still had periods of weakness. He and Evie had gone to bed early that night leaving the problem with who it was coming their way up to Captain Davisson.

James was standing watch just out of camp to the north when he saw a few people walking up to him. He stopped the small group but did not recognize Mia and the others. He allowed them to pass. There was no one else to stop and check them. With others walking around the large campfire no one challenged Mia as he walked right up to Scott's tent and opened fire into the side of it. A second later one of Evie's women took Mia down. Others disarmed him and held him down.

"Medic." Scott yelled. "Medic."

Others ran into the tent and found that Evie had been hit by three of the bullets in her upper leg. Scott had been shot once in he left hand. As the medics took care of Evie Scott stormed out of the tent with a pistol in hand.

"Who did this?" Scott yelled. Then he saw Mia being held on the ground. "Let'em up." he ordered those holding Mia down. "You shot Evie. Your punishment is death." Scott said as he raised his pistol and fired. Mia was dead.

Suddenly the other five started firing into the camp. Others in the camp opened fire down the highway and before long the gunfire stopped. As some of the Texicans went into the dark to find who had opened fire on the camp Scott checked on Evie. One of the medics grabbed Scott's arm and brought him back out of the tent and tended to his hand. The medic assured Scott that Evie would be okay.

Scott had been shot through the skin between his thumb and index finger. The medic patched him up. Seven others in camp had also been hit but none of their wounds were serious.

As Scott started to walk back into the tent he saw some of the Texicans bringing in three people that quickly recognized. He looked down at the body of the boy he shot and realized that he had shot Mia; although he did not know the boy's name. He was puzzled at this wondering why they were doing this.

"What are you kids doing?" Scott asked them.

"You killed our parents and we will kill you for doing that." The oldest girl said.

"Two more of them are down the road dead." James informed Scott.

"Where are the other children?" Scott asked.

"They went on to Teague." the girl answered again.

Scott took in a deep breath and let it out. Then he looked at Captain Bowers and said; "I will not have these ... people trying to kill us off. Take them down the road and execute them."

"Yes Sir." Bowers quickly answered.

Captain Bowers took six of his Texicans down the road with the prisoners and did his job. A few minutes later he returned and informed Scott that he carried out his duty.

"Thank you Captain." Scott said and then went back into the tent.

By this time the medic had removed two of the bullets in Evie's leg. She cringed when the medic pulled the third bullet out. Evie could see he worry in Scott's eyes and assured him that she would be okay. Scott shook his head up and down and then left the tent.

"I didn't come out here to kill kids." Scott told Captain James.

"You came out here to kill the enemy whether it is Black Muslims, MS-13 gang members, Mexicans, or white kids trying to kill you. They are then enemy and your job is to kill all of them ... Sir." James said.

"Please remind me to never piss you off." Scott commented.

"No problem Sir." James said with a big smile. Then he turned and walked away.

Later the medic told Scott that Evie would be just fine after a few days rest but she would not be walking anytime soon. Since the Texicans had no spe̍cial place to be going he decided to allow everyone to get a little more rest. They would wait at least a few days giving Evie time to rest as well. What Scott did not know was that another Mexican brigade commanded by Brigadier General Diego Lopez was in Franklin moving towards Marquez.

Lopez moved his brigade across the Rio Grand River just three weeks earlier and had met no serious fighting. However; between him and the town of Marquez was Newton's Militia. Months earlier Newton had a fight where his militia was nearly wiped out. He now had over six hundred soldiers all wanting to fight the Mexicans and free the new Republic of Texas. Unlike Sanchez, Lopez had a full brigade of four thousand men. Newton's six hundred soldiers was no match for Lopez's four thousand soldiers.

Newton took his militia to fight Lopez but quickly turned back when he saw that he was facing so many Mexicans. He was outnumbered about eight to one. Newton reached Marquez just in time for a few artillery rounds from Lopez to come down on his militiaman. In this one shelling alone Newton lost almost two hundred soldiers. Another one hundred ran off indifferent directions leaving his with just about three hundred soldiers.

Over the next few days Newton continued to run towards the town of Jewett. Every now and then Lopez would fire a few more artillery rounds killing and wounding even more of Newton's soldiers. When Newton's Militia came into Jewett on Highway 79 he continued to run He was trying to reach Buffalo as quickly as possible.

Having vehicles to carry men Lopez advanced quickly to where ever Newton was. Then his soldiers would engage Newton's Militia Killing even more of them. Finally Newton stopped in the town of Jewett to make a stand. He was being wiped out anyway so they might as well die fighting.

The Texicans waited four days and then broke camp and got ready to move out. Just as Lopez reached the northern part of Jewett the Texicans were also coming into town on Highway 39. The Texicans could not help but to hear all of the gunfire. Scott sent Battalion C ahead to find out what was going on.

Captain Davisson radioed back telling Scott what was going on. If they moved down onto Highway 79 they would have Lopez in a crossfire. Davisson could not see who Lopez was fighting but the Texicans had a good chance to overwhelm the Mexicans. Scott ordered the other Texicans ahead to fight. He sent Evie to the north to hit the Mexicans from the left flank. Unknown to Scott or Newton the people of the town were also firing from their homes. Lopez was catching it from all sides.

Lopez ordered a retreat to the east where his soldiers only had to face civilians in their homes. By time Lopez got out of town he had lost eleven hundred soldiers to death and another six hundred were wounded or captured. While Lopez ran for his life the Texicans took the six hundred prisoners and held them in the center of town.

The wounded on both sides were tended to. Then one of the Mexican soldiers that Scott had released earlier stood and yelled; "El Diablo … El Diablo."

Struck with fear the other prisoners jumped up and started to run in all directions. The Texicans opened fire killing almost all of them. Thirteen remained still alive. Seven were so badly wounded that they died later. Three others had their wounds tended to. The six that survived were taken to another parking lot and sat on the ground. That was when Newton walked up to Scott and tried to take over.

"You again." Newton yelled at Scott. "I'm in charge now."

"I don't know who you think you are but you're not in charge you son of a stupid whore." Scott yelled back at Newton.

"You're with that Texas Militia aren't you?"

"Texican Militia and we have kicked more Mexicans asses than you have." Scott reminded Newton.

Newton looked over the young Scott and said; I'll control my soldiers and you control your … boys."

"I have no desire to take over your group." Scott said. "My militia is big enough."

Scott and Newton talked for about thirty minutes and in all of that time Scott learned only one thing. Newton was a certifiable nut case. Newton had just under two hundred soldiers and Scott had four hundred seventy soldiers. Newton's men had been leaving him for a long time. He was such a bad commanding officer that he could not keep enough men to fight.

Scott walked away from Newton wondering how much longer he would live. Before long many of Newton's men were coming to Scott wanting to join the Texicans. That night most of Newton's men left Newton's Militia and joined the Texican Militia. When Newton came storming his way into the Texican camp he had his rifle raised at Scott.

"You're not taking my soldiers." he yelled at Scott. "I'm taking yours."

When Newton pointed his rifle at Scott two of the Texicans fired their M-16s at full auto. Newton was dead before his body hit the ground.

Scott turned to Newton's men and said; "You all can join us if you want. You don't have to."

"He never gave us a choice at anything." one of the women from Newton's Militia said. "You did everything he wanted or you got shot."

"Well I do have one rule." Scott said. Everyone in the Texican Militia can come and go as you wish but, as long as you are here you will obey my orders or I will have you shot."

Everyone that joined the Texican Militia agreed. Eleven of

them left the camp and went their own way. With others from Jewett joining during the night the Texican Militia grew to five hundred ninety three.

Chapter 7

The California Militia

Scott and his Texican Militia had become famous in not only the Republic of Texas but also in the rest of the United States, Mexico and South America. Americans were flooding over the northern Texas border to join the Texicans. UN troops shot on sight anyone they caught trying to cross into the Republic of Texas. The American president turned Communist dictator gave Texas and California back to Mexico and Scott's Texican Militia was making it hard for Mexico to get Texas. California on the other hand was full of Liberal Communist that happily excepted the Mexican rule.

The Texican Militia set up their tents and stayed in Jewett for six days. This gave Scott, Evie, and other wounded time to heal some. On the forth day Scott got word that a very large MS-13 gang had moved into Groesbeck and took over half of the town. Scott remembered how that town treated his militia the last time they came through there and wondered why they should go back.

The woman that escaped Groesbeck told Scott that this MS-13 gang had over three hundred members. They were raping the young women and many times girls as young as six. They were murdering many of those that lived there just to be killing someone. The woman told Scott that a Mexican brigade in Huntsville armed them all and gave them enough supplies to last a long time.

The town of Groesbeck had the MS-13 gang held back at Highway 14 but they would be running out of ammunition soon. The entire town would be lost if the Texicans did not get there as soon as possible. Evie and the other wounded were able to travel so Scott ordered the many camps in Jewett to break camp early on the fifth morning.

One of the trucks had been converted into a type of ambulance for carrying wounded. Evie and a few others that could not yet walk were loaded in the back of this truck which brought up the rear as the Texicans left Jewett.

Scott had Captain Davisson take the lead about half a mile in front of the rest of the Texicans. If they were ambushed then the other Texicans could advance and help hem out. Scott's Humvee took the lead of the main body of Texicans. They took Highway 39 out of town to the north. In a day or so they would turn west on Highway 164. Scott hoped to catch the MS-13 gang between the townspeople of Groesbeck and the advancing Texican Militia.

Because of a the ambulance truck breaking down three times it took the Texicans four days to reach Highway 164. Groesbeck was only a day or so to the west of there. As Scott lead the Texicans towards Groesbeck he sent Captain Davisson's Company C on to Groesbeck to check things out. Bowers' Company A moved up to the front with Scott and Evie's Company B took up the rear with the ambulance. James and his scavengers were scavenging for food and other supplies.

When Captain Davisson came up to the stockyard on the eastern side of Groesbeck he found many of the MS-13 gang there. A gun fight started killing thirteen of Davisson's men and wounding another four. All twenty three of the gang members were killed. Davisson called on his radio asking that the ambulance be brought to get the wounded.

Scott had Evie and the other wounded taken out of the ambulance and set aside where they would be safe. Then it was sent to Davisson to get the wounded there. Scott called back to Davisson and asked if he could get a few prisoners for questioning.

"I'll try Sir but they don't want to give up." Davisson said over his radio.

By this time the main body of MS-13 gang members heard about a small company killing their members at the Groesbeck stockyard. Their leader sent two platoons of their members to stop Davisson and his company. This time Davisson's men had plenty of things to hide behind and he only lost two men. He also captured four members of the gang.

The four MS-13 gang members were brought to the Groesbeck stockyard where they were told that El Diablo was waiting for them. While the four prisoners were being held on their knees in the stockyard parking lot Scott was trying something new. Earlier he had found some red clothing die. He wet a rag with the die and put it on his face, neck, arms, and hands. When he walked out in the sun he looked just like the devil himself.

As soon as the gang members saw Scott walking out of the building they tried to get away but their hands and feet were tied. Texicans holding them down with their feet did not help any either. The gang members yelled El Diablo and begged for mercy but no mercy was coming.

"Shut up." Scott yelled at the four Mexican men. Two of them had peed in their pants. They were scared out of their minds. "I am El Diablo and unless you talk I will be taking your souls back to Hell with me."

Suddenly one of he Mexican men yelled back at Scott. "You aren't shit. You're not El Diablo or nothing else."

Scott had the man gagged. Then he was laid on a wooden bench and tied down with his hands above his head. Scott walked over to a small campfire a few feet away and grabbed a tree limb. Holding the end that was not burning he had the Mexican's boots and socks removed. Then he lay the burning end on the bench against the Man's feet. The gang member tried to scream and move his feet but nothing was easing the pain of his feet being burned.

As the man's feet continued to burn Scott looked at the other three and started asking questions. For some reason they told El Diablo everything he wanted to know. They cried and continued to beg for mercy.

Scott removed the burning stick from the first man's feet. He had passed out from the pain. The bottoms of his feet were black with no skin left on them. In spots blood ran down to his heals. Scott had the man untied knowing that he was not going to run away. Then he pulled his pistol and shot one of the three others in the head. When he turned his pistol towards the other two they screamed and begged for mercy again. Scott slowly pulled his pistol back.

"You two are going to deliver a message to your leader." Scott insisted. "You two are going to take your friend back and then you're going to tell your friends that I am coming through town in the morning. I will burn any of hem that I see with the fires of Hell itself. Look at his feet. Now imagine the pain you will feel when your entire body looks like this."

The two men were released. This time they were not given food and water before leaving. As they helped the burned man to his feet he screamed from the pain. The man screamed with each step he took as his friends tried to hold him up. It took thirty minutes just to reach the road but it was important for the others to see what El Diablo had done to this man. He also wanted to make sure that the others knew that El Diablo was coming for the rest of them in the morning.

By time the three gang members were farther down the road it was getting dark. Scott had Captain Davisson keep his men at the stockyard. Captain Bowers and his company were moved just one quarter of a mile behind them. Then he went back to Evie and spent the rest of the night with her.

Scott learned a few things from the gang members. First of all there were about two hundred of hem farther into the town. The townspeople were still holding the gang off at Highway 14 but the gang members were running short on ammunition. This was all good news. With the Texicans outnumbering the gang almost three to one and with them running short of ammunition then an attack on the gang should be quick and easy. However; the gang members lied to Scott. There were about two hundred fifty of hem and they had plenty of ammunition. They also had plenty of RPGs.

When Scott got back to Evie he found her sitting by a campfire close to their tent. A folding chair was brought out of the tent for Scott and he sat beside Evie. They talked for hours before he helped her back inside the tent. The rest of the night was uneventful for all of the Texicans.

Scott got up about two hours before daylight the next morning. He talked with some of the Texicans there and then climbed in his Humvee to go back down to the stockyard. He was stopped while the medic changed he bandages on his hand. The medic told him that his hand was healing well. Only then did he leave.

Scott got out of the Humvee with a cup of coffee in hand. Half of the coffee was in his lap thanks to a Private that was just learning to drive. "Try to miss a few of those holes next time." he told his driver.

"I'm sorry Sir." the Private said.

Scott looked back at the Private with a smile. "That's okay. Don't worry about it."

Scott had the Texicans break camp and get ready for an assault on the MS-13 gang. He had Captain Bowers and his Company A move ahead of Captain Davisson. They would attack in two waves; first Company A and then Company C after them.

Evie had turned temporary command of Company B to Lieutenant Travis, a very capable woman. Scott had Company B fallow Company C as a third wave. James and his company stayed behind to guard the trucks and wounded. With about two hundred yards between Companies A, B, and C Scott gave the order to attack.

The three gang members that went back with one being burned very badly had a pronounced effect on the MS-13 gang members. At least fifty of hem skipped out of town before the Texicans got there. By this time only about one hundred MS-13 gang members remained in the eastern part of Groesbeck. They were about to be squeezed between the people of Groesbeck and the Texicans.

The last thing that Scott should have done was move himself

close to the fighting but, he did it anyway. He set up behind a pile of broken concrete two blocks from the main fighting. Using his 270 rifle he picked targets and fired. With every shot he sent another gang member to Hell where he belonged. After using the forty rounds that he took with him he returned to Evie.

The battle went on for hours. Slowly but surely the MS-13 gang lost more and more of its members. Unfortunately; the Texicans were loosing soldiers as well. The fighting went on until around three in the evening. That was when the remaining twenty one gang members surrendered.

With the MS-13 gang members defeated and prisoners captured Scott came into the town. The prisoners were moved to the railroad overpass over Highway 164. By time Scott got there the Sheriff was already taking credit for ending the gang's siege on the town. With Texicans all around the captured MS-13 members the sheriff even tried to take credit for their capture.

"Who the hell are you?" the sheriff asked Scott who was still wearing the red die.

Scott looked at his red arms and hands and then laughed. "Well … I'm El Diablo."

"You aren't El Shit." the sheriff said.

"Are you crazy?" one of he men from town asked the sheriff. "El Diablo is the one that is going to save the Republic of Texas if anyone does."

Others in the crowd also started going against the sheriff until he left with two or three of his followers. When the others in the town found out that it was El Diablo that saved them they came out with food, wine, and even a few gallons of peach brandy moonshine.

All but seven of the MS-13 gang were killed with four of the seven badly wounded. The Texicans lost twenty two and had another thirty nine wounded. With so many wounded Scott had the Texicans stay there for a few more days. The Texican Militia set up camp in a grocery store parking lot and in nearby grass.

The Texican Militia were also running short on supplies so Scott tried to call Central Command in Dallas but they were to far away for the hand held radio. A few seconds after trying to reach Central Command someone else came back to Scott on the radio.

"This is KG5EYU calling the man asking for Central Command." a man's voice came over the radio. "Who are you?"

"This is El Diablo ... I mean Major Staninski of the Texican Militia." Scott told the man.

"Are you that group that just saved Groesbeck from the MS-13 gang?" the man asked.

"Yes Sir we are."

"Well heck boy." the man added. "I'm less than half a mile from you."

Come to find out the man had a HAM radio base station and was able to reach Central Command with his radio. Scott went to meet the man. When they got to his home an old man walked out.

The old man's name was Darren Poke. He walked out of his garage when Scott drove up in his Humvee. Darren was an Extra Class HAM radio operator not that having an operator's licenses mattered anymore. He was sixty eight years old and had lived in Groesbeck all of his life. Darren's wife Margie asked Scott and his Captains to stay for dinner but Scott turned her down. He knew that the MS-13 gang had taken most of the food in town before they were forced back to Highway 14. Later he did send a case of MREs back to Darren and Margie for helping him get in contact with Central Command.

Central Command would fly supplies out to the Texicans the next morning. The target for the drop was the Highway 164 and Highway 14 crossroads in downtown Groesbeck. They would be getting everything from MREs to ammunition but fuel for the Humvee and trucks they would have to find on their own. Fuel was becoming harder and harder to find.

The next morning Darren called Scott on his radio and said that the aircraft with their supplies just left Dallas. An hour later the aircraft was close enough to call Scott on his hand held radio. They would be dropping seven large pallets of supplies in two minutes. The plane flew right over Highway 14 heading south.

Every pallet landed on the highway but no one considered the power lines and stop lights. There was no electricity running through the lines but they still hung up in the parachute cords. None of the supplies was lost.

As the plane dropped the supplies the pilot told Scott that the Texican Militia was being considered the most important militia in the Republic of Texas. The Texicans had destroyed one Mexican Battalion and one Brigade not to mention two conflicts with Black Muslims and at least two conflicts with large MS-13 gangs. No other militia in the republic of Texas had done so much to free the Republic of Texas. Then the pilot told Scott something that he was very happy to hear. Central Command would be keeping the Texican Militia supplied from then on.

Scott had the trucks brought up and the supplies loaded into them. The ambulance truck had to give up two cots to hold the rest of the supplies. By this time Evie was already walking around and carrying her rifle. She had been carrying an M-16 but now carried an M-14 with a scope. It had been set up as a sniper's rifle. Before being wounded she was getting better as a sniper and now talked with Scott about fighting beside him as two snipers.

Scott thought about what Evie asked. He needed her with the other women in her company but, if he did do as she asked then he could keep her safer. She would be with him and not be going into any battles.

Scott had Evie choose a woman in her Company B to take over the company. After thinking about it for a while she chose Lieutenant Quinn. Quinn was a thirty two year old woman that had proven herself many times in the past. Evie and Quinn had been friends for many years before the Mexican invasion.

The next morning Lieutenant Quinn was called to Scott's tent. She was so nervous thinking that she was in trouble for something she had done or, not done. Scott and Evie talked with her for awhile and then Scott promoted her to Captain of Company B.

Everyone had expected this to happen sooner or later. They

had not kept their relationship a secret. However many did not think that Eve should keep her rank of Captain. Hearing this around camp Evie gave up her rank. From then on she was just Scott's woman.

Although the two had been sleeping together for a few weeks they had not had any sex. The next morning every one knew that, that had changed when Scott got up with a smile on his face. Scott never got up with a smile on his face.

Many of the men and women of the Texican Militia had started sleeping together before Scott and Evie. Scott had no problem as long as there were no men with men or women with women.

In the supplies was a long message letting Scott know what had been going on around in the Republic of Texas. A few of he reports were about Scott and his Texican Militia. He did learn that a large militia in far west Texas wiped out another Mexican Brigade. Major Boling of the 7th Militia surrounded the Mexicans Brigade. When the Mexicans chose to die fighting Boling obliged him and wiped them out in just a few hours.

The dictator president of the United States tried many times to send UN troops across the border into the Republic of Texas to help the Mexicans but, the Texas troops guarding the border on the Texas side held them off. These Texas troops were a mixture of US troops that were sent into Texas before the UN troops were sent and militias and other volunteers from surrounding states. The southern border with Mexico was guarded by the Texas National Guard and other National Guardsmen from surrounding states. This was why the main area inside the Republic of Texas was defended by militias in the Republic Texas and sometimes militias from other states.

A militia out of California went through Mexico and then crossed the Rio Grand River into the Republic of Texas. They were young liberal/communist men and women that did not agree with anyone fighting against the Mexican government. California had surrendered everything what the Mexican government moved troops into the state. They happily excepted their state being given to Mexico and fought anyone that resisted it.

Mexico had got with the men and women of this militia and agreed to supply them with everything they needed if they would go into the Republic of Texas and fight them. Mostly made up of young people the California Militia went into the Republic of Texas for one reason. They were to destroy the Texican Militia. Over one hundred young but seasoned Mexican soldiers went with the California Militia posing as Americans.

Looking like a new Texas militia the California militia was never stopped or challenged when they crossed the Mexican border into the Republic of Texas. As they marched through Mexico on their way to the border with the republic they grew in strength. By time they crossed the border into the republic they were five hundred twenty strong.

The men that ran the California Militia was called Major David Morris. The rank of Major was given to him by the Mexican government.

Major Morris made a big mistake after crossing into the Republic of Texas. His hatred for those in the Republic of Texas that resisted the Mexican rule was so great that it showed as he marched his militia northward. Instead of being nice to the cities and small towns he treated them with contempt. His men quite often raped the women of towns they passed through. Instead of asking for food his militia took what ever they wanted. By time he reached Houston he was hated just as much as any Mexican Brigade coming through.

By time Major Morris had reached Huntsville Scott knew that the Major's militia was not a regular militia but one that came to get him. He knew that they were out of California and that they came to wipe out the Texican Militia. Scott could not understand how a militia was suppose to wipe out his militia when one Mexican Battalion and one Brigade could not do it. Then he realized that Morris had made this mistake of giving away his true feelings as he moved north.

One night as Scott and Evie sat by their campfire she reminded him that the California was coming after him.

“I know and I’ve been thinking about it.” Scott told her as she hung onto his arm. “Sun Tzu said that we should choose where to fight our battles. I haven’t been doing that.”

Scott had been a reader of Sun Tzu’s teachings of The Art of War for many years. But until now he had not used what he learned. Sun Tzu’s teachings was required reading at most military academies and even large businesses. It has been said that if you fallow Sun Tzu’s teachings you will never fail.

What Scott needed to do was lure Morris into an ambush; a place where the Texicans would have defenses but Morris and his militia would not. After a while Scott finally thought of the perfect place for an ambush.

The next morning Scott had the Texicans break camp and head for the town of Thorton. Then he sent ten of the Texicans out to Marquez, Jewett, and Centerville to tell everyone that the Texican Militia was seen in Kosse. When the California Militia came through Centreville Morris got the word. Scott’s plan was started.

Two weeks after the Texicans reached Thorton the California Militia was passing through Marquez on Highway 7. As Major Morris moved his militia through Marquez they were ambushed. Scott had set up the ambush just west of Marquez but if was not anal lout attack. It was just the first of many small ambushes to demoralize Morris’ militia. Scott had set up two more ambushes on Highway 79 between Marquez and Kosse. By time Morris and his California Militia reached Kosse they had lost eighty of their militia members. Morris only had four hundred and fifty left. The Texicans on the other hand only lost three members.

While in Kosse Morris got word that the Texican Militia was running from him. This of course was just part of the plan. He was also told that many in the Texican Militia had deserted leaving only one hundred fifty to fight. This was just another lie to lure Morris into the trap. Morris did not want the Texicans to get away so he ordered his militia to fallow the Texicans north on Highway 14 to Groesbeck. They needed rest but, Morris wanted

the Texican Militia so bad that he denied them that rest.

Major Morris took his four hundred fifty strong militia towards Groesbeck to fight another militia that he thought was only one hundred fifty strong. The truth was that the Texicans were still five hundred fifty three strong. With the Texican Militia only having one hundred more fighters than the California Militia the trap was about to be sprung.

Chapter 8

Groesbeck

Scott was getting everything he had planned but something told him to slow down some. Scouts told him that the California Militia was on their way up Highway 14 to catch the Texicans in Groesbeck. However they were not in Groesbeck. The Texican Militia had set up a final ambush on Highway 14 in Thorton. There they railroad tracks ran along beside the highway on its eastern side. The Texicans were lined up on the eastern side of the tracks using them as cover.

Morris was pushing his militia hard. By time they reached Thorton they were to tired to fight. It was already dark so Morris did not even check out the town of Thorton as they passed by. Then suddenly a flare flew up high in the air and Morris knew that he had been had.

Over four hundred rifles along the railroad tracks started firing at one time. The other sixty three of the Texican Militia brought up the rear behind the California Militia on Highway 14 catching Morris and his militia in a kind of two way crossfire. Within ten minutes the battle was over. Being to tired to fight all but forty two of the California Militia were killed or badly wounded. The others were captured including Major Morris himself.

Scott had the prisoners sit in the middle of highway 14 under guard. Seeing how tired they were he allowed them to sleep if they wanted. Scott retired to the main Camp close to his tent. As he sat by the campfire Evie sat beside him. Sliding her arm between his arm and body she hung on tight.

"You okay Babe?" Scott asked Evie.

Evie took in a deep breath and let it out. "Yeah I'm okay."

As the two sat by the fire a cold front came through. It was mid December and it had not really been cold yet. When the rain hit they both went into their tent. Scott wrote in his journal until Evie complained about him not being in the bed keeping her warm. A few minutes later he finished his writing and went to bed.

As the night went on the rain turned to sleet and then snow. The sleet fell for about two hours covering everything. Some of the tents caved in with the weight of the sleet but the Texicans made do. Scott had the camp guard use a broom to sweep off their tent every now and then. By time Scott got up the next morning there was three feet of snow on top of about one foot of sleet.

With plenty of dead trees around Scott had the campfire built up to help melt off some of the snow around the camp. Evie got up and made some coffee.

"What are you doing up?" Scott asked Evie.

"Well my man needs coffee." she advised him.

Scott smiled as she had never referred to him as her man before. Then he looked to his left at some of the men smiling at what she called him.

"Oh shut up." Scott jokingly said. After getting a cup of the coffee he took it out to seethe prisoners. They had no fire so Scott allowed them to get firewood and build one. A few minutes later he prisoners were very thankful for the blazing fire.

"We had more prisoners didn't we?" Scott asked one of the Texicans watching the prisoners.

"Yes Sir." a freshly promoted Corporal said. "The wounded were moved to a church down the road. There were twenty two of them Sir."

Before leaving the prisoners Scott had food brought out for the prisoners. Cold MREs was all they had but at least the prisoners were fed and given water. After returning to get more coffee he and Evie went to the church to see the wounded prisoners.

Two guards stood watch outside the church's main door. Three more stood watch one both sides where a prisoner could break a window and escape. Two more stood watch at the back door.

Scott, Evie, and the three Captains walked through the front door as it opened for them. The Captains stood ready to fire their rifles if any of the prisoners tried attacking Scott. Scott stopped and talked with each of the wounded. Then he finally came to Major Morris.

"I'm told that you're Major Morris." Scott said. With a bullet in the right side of his chest Morris did not feel like talking. "Well don't worry. We'll take care of you and your militia members."

"What's gon'a happen to us?" the woman beside Morris asked.

"You his woman?" Scott asked her.

The woman made a disgusting face. "I don't think so."

Scott stepped back some and said; "You're all going to be taken to Dallas where you'll be held as prisoners of war. You'll spend the rest of your lives there."

Evie looked at the woman and asked; "Do I know you?"

"I don't know anyone from this filthy state." the woman said.

"We are not a state." Evie smarted back to her. "We are a Republic of Texas."

"You're not shit Bitch." the woman yelled.

Evie stood, turned her rifle towards the woman and looked at her hard.

"Go ahead and shoot me Bitch." the woman dared Evie so Evie obliged her and pulled the trigger.

Others jumped back. Then Evie looked at Scott and said; "Well … she asked me to."

Scott took in a deep breath and let it out. Then he turned and left the church. Evie and the three Captains fallowed him outside.

"I need volunteers … about thirty." Scott said. "The others need to go home for a week or so and then come back."

"What do you mean?" Evie asked.

Scott turned and looked at his three Captains. "I need thirty volunteers to go with me and take these prisoners to Dallas."

Scott said. There is no reason why the others can not go home for awhile but return. We still have work to do."

"Ten from each company should do." Bowers said. "But wouldn't twenty be enough?"

Scott thought for a moment. "Twenty would be just fine."

All three Captains left and talked with their Texicans. By the next morning Scott had his twenty volunteers. Almost all of the Texicans volunteered but twenty were chosen mainly because hey had no families or homes to go to. Scott had all of the Texicans gather together for him to speak to.

"I have volunteers to take these prisoners to Dallas but there is no reason why the rest of you cannot go home for awhile and rest." Scott told the Texicans. "It will take a week to get to Dallas and another week to get back. I need all of you to return to this spot in three weeks."

"What if we don't want to come back." a woman yelled out. "Some of us are tired of fighting."

"All of us are tired of fighting." Scott told them all. "Let's see how tired you are when they come to your home and rape you and your daughters. Let's see how tardyon are when they come and take all the food you have left." Scott added as he looked around. "We are a militia. You can come and go as you wish. Those of you that want to continue fighting be back here in three weeks. Now be careful and ... I hope you all come back. Bring friends if you can."

Scott had the wounded prisoners loaded in the trucks. The other prisoners would walk but so would the Texicans watching them. As they left Thorton Scott looked back. The other Texicans had already left for their homes. No more than twenty people were left in Thorton but they were out on the road seeing Scott and he others off. He waved at them and they waved back. Then he turned and took the prisoners out of town.

Scott took the prisoners north to Groesbeck where he met the same blockade but this time they allowed the Texicans through. As they went through town a man stood beside the road and stopped Scott.

"Ha Major." the man said. "I'm the new Sheriff of Groesbeck. I'm Sheriff Gibbins."

Scott halted everyone and shook Sheriff Gibbins' hand. He told Gibbins what he was doing and the sheriff asked if he could walk with Scott until they were out of town. Scott agreed.

The two men talked until they got to the blockade Then the sheriff invited Scott to stay for Groesbeck's New year's calibration that night. Christmas had come and gone without Scott realizing it. The prisoners could be kept overnight in a nearby warehouse. Scott thought about the offer and Evie also wanted to stay. Scott agreed so the prisoners were taken to the warehouse where only four guards would be needed during the night. The Sheriff even offered to feed the prisoners.

Ten of the Texicans agreed to stay with the warehouse and guard it over he night. Scott, Evie, and the other ten Texicans were taken to a motel where they were set up for the night. The Sheriff would return that evening to take them all to the celebration.

As Scott walked around the motel room Evie asked what was wrong. She could see that he was deep in thought.

"Something's wrong with this." Scott said.

"With what." Evie asked.

Scott walked to the rooms that the other ten Texicans were in and asked them what they thought. Even they agreed that something was not quite right but they could not figure it out. Then there was a knock on the motel room door.

One of the Texicans opened the door only to find a rifle in his face. The armed men pushed their way into the room and grabbed all of the Texicans' firearms. Then Gibbins stepped in the room.

"Oh good." Gibbins said to Scott. "You're here."

"What's going on Gibbins?" Scott asked him.

"Well... it's like this." Gibbins said. " The city of Groesbeck had a town meeting last week and we had a long talk about what we want. We finally came to at least one conclusion. We want to be Americans not part of the Republic of Texas."

"So why are you holding us?" Scott asked.

"You're soldiers for the Republic of Texas. Now we have no plans to hurt any of you but you will fallow my orders or you will be shot."

"If you're not planning to hurt us then what are you doing?" Scott asked.

"As we speak your prisoners are being released and you will be put there ... but only for two days. Then we will release all of you as well."

Scott and the others in that room were taken outside where the other Texicans were waiting. Evie ran to Scott and hugged him out of fear. Scott told the other Texicans not to resist and they would not be harmed. They were taken four blocks away to the warehouse where the California Militia prisoners were standing outside.

As Scott and the others walked inside the warehouse Scott noticed others from the town that were in there including Darren poke. He walked over to Poke to find out what happened.

"Well it's simple." Poke said. "At the town meeting about ninety percent of the people agreed to be Americans and have nothing to do with the Republic of Texas. Then those of us that were all for the Republic of Texas was arrested and thrown into the county jail. About an hour ago we were moved to this warehouse."

"Why are you smiling?" Scott wanted to know.

"How ironic it is that this is my warehouse." Poke admitted and then laughed. "I just bought it a few months ago in an auction.

"Did they take your radio?" Scott asked.

"Not really." Poke said and then looked down. "They burned my home down." He looked up at Scott and added; "Pretty sure the radio looks like hell now."

The California Militia prisoners were given any of the Texicans' weapons that they needed. Groesbeck did not want to be under Mexican rule either so the California Militia members were taken to the southern blockade and released. They were also given the two trucks that the Texicans had for transporting their wounded. Sheriff Gibbins kept Scott's Humvee for himself.

The sheriff kept his word and fed and watered the Texicans three times a day. On the morning the door opened. Scott could see many armed people of Groesbeck standing outside. Each Texican was given two days of food and a full canteen of water. Then they were taken to the eastern blockade on Highway 164.

"Well good luck Major." Gibbins said. "But if you come back we will kill every one of you."

Scott lead the Texicans out of town and about one mile away when he stopped out of sight of the sheriff.

"No matter which direction we go we will be out of food in about two days. Hopefully the people of Donie would give them more food and then they would go to Dallas and rearm. Then they would probably come back to Groesbeck and take the town over.

It took nine days to reach Dallas. The Texicans had nothing as those in Groesbeck gave everything to the California Militia. When Scott told Central Command about this the Colonel was furious. He instantly ordered a bombing of he town but he also ordered the pilots to leave he warehouse standing.

Scott spent two full days answering questions from Central Command. Then he and the Texican Militia was re-supplied with one order from Command. Go back to Groesbeck and reclaim the town for the Republic of Texas. After gaining control of the town of Groesbeck the Texicans were to hunt down Morris and his California Militia and totally destroy them.

Scott was given everything that the Texicans got last time including two trucks and one Humvee. All of the Texicans were armed with new M-16s and four magazines. In the back of he trucks were twenty cases of .223 ammunition and a few explosives. The second truck was almost full of MREs. All of the Texicans were cold weather gear and extra gear was added to the trucks for those that went to see their families.

Scott knew that he could not go through Groesbeck yet with half of the Texicans on the other side in Thorton. Therefore; he gave the Humvee to five Texicans and sent them straight to Marquez where they would go to Kosse from there. Then they would go to Thorton and wait for the others and have them wait until he and the others got there. Scott and the others would travel the same rout and get to Thorton as quickly as possible.

The Texicans could have reached eastern Groesbeck in just over a week but having to go around to get to Thorton cast them sometime. It took ten days for the five to get to Thorton and keep the others there. Scott and the other Texicans drove into Thorton five days later.

As Scott and the others drove into Thorton they saw that the Texicans there had set up a blockade of their own. Evidentially those that went home did some recruiting. That night Scott learned that the Texican Militia was seven hundred twenty three strong. They had never been so large.

That night Scott talked with his Captains and planned an attack on Groesbeck. By midnight they finished and Scott went to his campfire to rest before going to bed. Evie brought out an MRE for him and sat beside him as he ate. He told her everything that they were to do in the attack on Groesbeck but she already knew. As he continued to tell her she realized that he was mainly going over the plans. Telling her was just a way of doing it without talking to himself. That would not have looked good to the others.

Finally Scott went into the tent where he sat in a chair. After Evie closed the flaps on the tent she got a bowl of water and a rag and bathed her man. Then they went to bed.

The next morning the Captains briefed their Texicans on the attack. The Texicans would break camp after eating breakfast and then they would be off for the southern side of Groesbeck.

The bombings ordered by Central Command was supposed to have taken out the southern blockade in Groesbeck but that was done two weeks earlier. Knowing that those that supported the republic of Texas were in the warehouse their second targets were the homes and of course City Hall.

On the seconding after leaving Thorton the Texicans came

within one mile of the southern blockade of Groesbeck. Being close enough for the guards at the southern blockade to seethe fires but out of range of any rifles Scott ordered at least fifty campfires built and had them spread out over a large distance on the highway and on both sides of the highway. From that distance it looked like a large army was coming the next day.

Scott also sent out Captain Davisson and his Company C ahead to capture anyone coming from Groesbeck trying to find out anything. Lieutenant Parker of the 3rd. Platoon would get closer and have his men take pop shots at the blockade every now and then.

All through the night Scott and the others could hear a shot here and there; never from the same spot. Every time a round was fired those in the camp laughed loud enough that those in Groesbeck could hear. By time morning came those in the city of Groesbeck were half out of their minds with fear.

As the eastern blockade was full of men and women getting ready to fight they looked over the small hills in the distance. It seemed as though the hills themselves were moving. Suddenly about two hundred yards from the blockade the hills stopped moving. As the Blockade guards looked closer they saw a wall of soldiers at least three hundred men wide.

Scott gave the order and all three hundred Texicans fired at one shot. Then three LAWs rocket flew over the line of Texicans and hit the blockade. There was no blockade to speak of after that.

The Texicans fired only one shot but they stood ready to give those in Groesbeck a lot more. A few minutes later more of the people of Groesbeck came to help and started firing at the Texicans. That was when Scott gave the order to move in.

The people of Groesbeck were great at building blockades on the four highways coming into town but they only had foot patrols between those blockades. The blockades were just for show and nothing more. While Lieutenant Davisson was close to the blockade the night before he saw this.

Before Scott advanced the Texicans he moved his company

to the west side of Highway 14 and took the far away from the highway so they would not be seen. This was done before daylight. Davisson moved his Texicans into town just inside the western blockade so they never saw the Texicans until they were attacked. Then they moved northward through the western side town. After a few blocks they spread out over five streets and moved east right through the main part of town. While Scott was keeping almost all of the people of Groesbeck busy at the southern blockade that no longer existed Davisson was wiping out those in town.

By time Scott's Texicans moved past the southern blockade they could see Davisson's company in the center of town. They turned to the north on Highway 14 and took out the northern blockade. Scott sent Captain Quinn's Company B of women to take out the eastern blockade.

While Scott sat on a bench in the middle of town Darren Poke walked up to him. Scott asked if he would like to be in charge of the rounding up of all the townspeople that hated the Republic of Texas. He excepted the job.

"Now when we leave I can't leave anyone here to help you." Scott told Poke. "We have to chase down that California Militia.

"I heard they went down to Marquez and settled in." Poke said. "Don't know for sure though."

"We'll find those Bastards." Scott said. "I'll find them."

Twenty eight people from Groesbeck that hated the Republic of Texas were rounded up that night. Another ninety seven were killed in the battle. Another twelve would not come out of their homes so they were simply burned alive in their homes. The twenty eight captured ones were kept over night in warehouse that the Texicans were kept in. Forty one of the townspeople wanted the Republic of Texas.

The next morning the prisoners were given a trial. They were all charged with Treason. All of them were found guilty and sentenced to death. Eager to get after the California Militia Scott had them all shot right there beside the warehouse.

The Texicans spent the night one mile south of Groesbeck

where their gear was left. That night Scott sat on a log by the campfire tending to a scrape on his hand that was bleeding some. As with most nights Evie brought out a MRE for him to eat. After talking twosome he Texicans for a while he went into the tent where Evie bathed him again. Then they went to bed where Evie was hoping to do a little more than just talk. But when she rolled over she saw that Scott was already asleep. With a big smile she lay her head down on her pillow and fell asleep. He was still her man and that was all that mattered.

Chapter 9

The Decision

Scott decided to allow the Texicans to rest a few days before heading out to find the California Militia. That first morning after taking over Groesbeck was spent with no one saying much. He did not know why everyone was so quiet but for him it was just because he was so tired. There was one more thing that bothered him. He was so angry with those in Groesbeck and the California Militia that he forgot to show any mercy as God told him to do.

It seemed as though the vicious behavior that the other Texicans showed in the killing all of the people that did not want to be apart of the Republic of Texas bothered many of the others as well. Who were these people that made up the Texican Militia? They were just people that wanted more than what the United States was giving them. They did not want a Communist Dictator for their president. They wanted someone like President Davis of the new Republic of Texas.

President Davis was an all out country boy. Raised in the hill country of central Texas he learned the importance of knowing how to hunt and fish. He was a full believer in the saying *"Give a man a fish and you feed him one time. Teach a man to fish and he will eat all of his life."* He was no stranger to work while the liberal communist want everything given to them. Standing at just over six feet tall he was a man among men. As the Governor of Texas he spoke against the liberal communist views of the United States President. Once the US President gave Texas to Mexico Governor Davis fought for Texas to become the new Republic of Texas and excepted the office of President of the new Republic of Texas.

Scott was much like Davis. He did not mind hard work. He

could hunt and fish, clean the fish or animal and even cook it later. Survival was a matter of life as he learned how to survive off of the grid. It was no wonder that he would become the leader of the most powerful militia in the Republic of Texas.

When the Texicans broke camp and left they headed south on Highway 14 to the town of Kosse. Once there they stayed the rest of that day and all that night. Scott spoke to many of the people who had heard about the California Militia being in Marquez. Those living in Kosse loved to see their friends again and were happy to have their protection even if it was just for the one night.

The people of Kosse were mostly older people. Many of their younger people had joined a militia with most of them joined the Texicans. There was just so much protection that the older people can do. They all had what it took in their hearts but they moved slower and were only able to do some things. With some of them being Veterans they did well but, against even a small militia they would not do well.

Some of the people of Kosse told Scott that the California Militia was still in Marquez but most of them had heard that the militia had moved south. The Texicans would just have to go and find out.

He next morning the Texicans ate their breakfast early and broke camp before daylight. By time the sun was coming up the trucks were loaded and they were heading east on Highway 7 to Marquez.

The California Militia had moved on to the town of Flynn. There they learned for a couple of spies they sent out that the Texican Militia was after them again. Major Morris of the California Militia still had Scott's Humvee and did not want to give it back. He also knew that his militia was not strong enough to fight the Texicans. He needed more soldiers and weapons. He also knew that if he could talk to the impressionable young people then he might get the soldiers. Finding weapons would Ben problem.

In the middle of he night Morris broke camp and moved his

militia out of Flynn. His target was the young people in Madisonville. Leaving at night left the few people in Flynn not knowing which direction they went.

By time the Texicans reached Marquez Major Morris was almost in Madisonville. The day that the Texicans came into Marquez there was hardly anyone around. They set up camp on all four corners of the crossing highways of 79 and 7.

Two couples walked up and introduced themselves as homeless people having lost their homes to a Mexican Brigade that came through a few months earlier. They told Scott that a large group of people calling themselves the California Militia came through and move on towards Centerville. What Scott did not know was that these four people were spies sent out by Major Morris to purposely mislead the Texicans.

The next morning the Texicans broke camp and headed for Centerville. Along the way Scott talked to people that were walking the other direction and none of them had seen any large group for many weeks. Either Major Morris moved through the area sooner than he thought or these people just did notate talk. Either way; something was wrong.

The next day the Texicans came to the tiny town of Robbins. This town consisted of one store on the corner of Highway 39 and Highway 7 and that was it. In the store parking lot a small tent was set up. This was a common thing to see as many had lost their homes to the Mexicans. As Scott talked to the couple and their daughter the Texicans set up camp for the night.

The man and woman told Scott about a large group of people moving north on Highway 39 towards Jewett. The problem was that these people were also spies set there by Major Morris to misdirect the Texicans in the wrong direction. While Scott was chasing a false trail Morris was recruiting young people in Madisonville. Scott did not realize that he had been mislead until he got to Jewett.

The spies that Major Morris used were good at what they did. Scott was sure that Morris was proud of them. The last couple even had a young girl with them so they looked like any other family trying to survive.

No one in Jewett had seen any large group of people coming through for over two months and they were a Mexican Brigade. The Texicans had already taken care of them. Scott realized that the spies had mislead him and the Texican Militia towards Jewett. That meant that Morris and his California Militia had to be in the other direction but, where?

The next day Scott ad the Texicans break camp again. As the sun came up the weather started turning colder. By time the Texicans were moving out a storm hit. At first it only rained but as it got colder the rain turned to sleet and then snow. Now the Texicans were wet from the rain and freezing because it was close to freezing. When they reached the school Scott thought that it would be best to set up camp and allow everyone to get dry and warm. The last things he needed was a bunch of fighters that were to sick to fight.

By the next morning at least thirty percent of his Texicans were already sick. Scott knew that they had to stay there for a few days and allow his militia to heal up. It seemed that the older fighters were the ones that got sick so Scott sent out the younger ones to cut wood for the campfires.

In the meantime Morris continued to recruit young people in Madisonville. They got word into Huntsville causing the young people there to come into Madisonville. Anyone in Madisonville that resisted was shot on sight by the young people that were looking for an answer. Madisonville had their own militia that only protected the city but, the young soldiers in the California Militia almost completely wiped them out.

Before long word got out to the young people in other towns of this new way of thinking that Mexican rule was the answer. Another MS-13 gang out of east Texas came to Madisonville and volunteered to be Morris' personal guards. However; Morris used them as hit men not guards. There job was to shut anyone up that spoke against this new movement.

This MS-13 gang was called Morris' Guards. They were a savage bunch of mostly Mexicans. None of the members of the

California Militia could join them unless they were of Hispanic decent. Even then Morris needed more in the militia than in his Guards. Many Mexicans in the California Militia could not join Morris' Guards because they simply were not needed.

The Texicans stayed at the school for over a week. Seven of them were still sick and they lost three to pneumonia. The seven did not have pneumonia so Scott had them loaded into one truck that had been converted into another ambulance. A small coal burning cast iron stove burned wood to keep it warm for the sick. A hole was cut in the canvas top of the truck for the chimney. The rest of the Texicans broke camp and left the school. They were on their way back to Robbins. From there Scott had no idea which way to go.

By time the Texicans reached Robbins the California Militia had grown to two hundred five strong. Most of these were confused young people that thought they had the perfect idea as to what Texas should do. They had no idea what living under Mexican rule would be like but, they really believed that this new movement was the answer.

Scott had no idea that the California Militia was in Madisonville and that they were doing any recruiting. Once they got to Robbins they heard from a few people that the California Militia were in Madisonville. Scott did not know if he should trust this news as the last couple there had mislead him. He had the Texicans set up camp while he would spend the next day or so talking to others. Surely Morris had not sent that many spies to misdirect him.

By the next night Scott had talked to, to many people that mentioned a large group of people in Madisonville recruiting young people. He was told that these young people were killing anyone that disagreed with them and that some MS-13 gang members were also there. Then finally someone came by that heard that a man named Morris was running things in Madisonville. Finally Scott knew which way to go next.

The next morning the Texicans broke camp and headed towards Centerville. As they traveled Scott continued to talk to people heading the other direction and most of them mentioned a group of mostly young people from all around that was forming a new type of movement. This movement was in favor of Mexico taking over the Republic of Texas.

By time the Texicans got to Centerville they were tired. Scott had made the mistake of pushing them too hard. Scott knew that he could not keep pushing everyone if he wanted them to be able to fight. As soon as they crossed over Interstate 45 they were stopped by a large, well armed group.

Scott talked to those from the city for awhile. They also told him about Major Morris being in Madisonville. They had heard about the Texican Militia but still did not want to just trust them. Scott took the Texicans back across Interstate 45 and set up camp for the night. They would break camp and move south the next morning. That was the plan anyway.

The next morning people from the city of Centerville came out to them with food and other things they might need. Much like Madisonville the people of Centerville had their own militia that just took care of the city. The mayor of Centerville came out and talked with Scott.

The mayor told Scott that many of the young people in the city had left to hear the teachings of a Major Morris in Madisonville. Even a few young people from Buffalo and Fairfield had passed through Centerville on their way to hear more about this new movement. Scott was nostril he wanted to attack the California Militia now. Fighting a militia was one thing but fighting a movement could get them all killed. Scott learned something else as well.

The California Militia had been set up in the Walmart parking lot on the north side of town. Scott had no idea how large the militia was but by this time they had grown even more to be three hundred ninety strong. Scott felt bad about having to kill hundreds of confused kids but this movement had to be stopped as soon as possible. This movement was quickly becoming a cult of religion. The last thing that the Republic of Texas needed was a large cult movement. Hopefully the Texicans would wipe out the California Militia and this cult movement at the same time.

When the Texicans moved out of Centerville Scott had no idea that the California Militia had grown to just over four hundred and continued to grow by the day. Scott decided to send in a couple of his own spies. He chose Bill and Nancy Doman. They were husband and wife but most fall they looked younger than they were. Bill was thirty two but looked around twenty. Nancy was thirty but looked almost like a teen.

Scott stopped his Texicans about half way to Madisonville while his two spies continued on to their objective. Bill and Nancy were to learn all they could and then return to Scott in four days. Two days later they reached a partial blockade on the interstate. They told the guards that they had heard about a new movement and wanted to learn more. They were allowed to pass.

Bill and Nancy spent three days in Madisonville and then left that night out of fear. If the militia members even thought that a person was not serious about joining then that person was shot. A few young people were killed every day. So they would not bee seen they left at night. When they got to the blockade they took to the woods and passed it by and then came back out on the interstate.

An almost full moon lit their way on the interstate until they reached the Texican guards. Then they were taken to Scott's campfire where they would wait until he woke up. He commotion outside the tent woke Scott up so he got up and came outside. He sat at the campfire and listened to Bill and Nancy for two hours asking questions from time to time. When the two were finished with their report they went to a tent that had been set up for them. Being about one hour before daylight Scott just stayed up.

There was one more thing that bothered Scott. The California Militia was as big or bigger than the Texican Militia. This fight could go either way. The Texicans on the interstate turned back any young people that came out of the north. However; they could not stop those coming from the other directions. The California Militia was growing by the minute so the Texicans had to do something now.

"Father, I need your help again. I am about to go into battle against almost all kids. I am about to be killing children that think they know it all. They really believe that Mexican rule over Texas is best. Please show me what to do Lord. Amen."

As the Texican Militia broke camp Scott pondered an idea. These kids had probably not seen much death. If the Texicans could show them so much death at one time then they might loose the stomach to fight. It was worth a try.

Before leaving the area Scott called for his Captains and told them what he was wanting to do. Of course much of want he wanted depended on what the situation looked like when they got to the blockade. When the Texicans got within one mile of Madisonville Scott stopped everyone. Then he spread out Company A to his left and Company to his right. Company B would bring up the rear in the center if and when any shooting started. He would drop back behind Company B.

Scott took the Texicans just close enough to the blockade so that they were out of range of most rifles. Then he had them just stand there in plane sight but as quiet as possible. None of the Texicans moved or walked around. From the blockade they looked like a wall stretching from onside the interstate and into the woods to the other side and into those woods. They were a frightening sight.

The Texicans just stood there until it got dark. Then Scott had them stand ready as they slowly walked forward. The Texicans had walked another two hundred yards when Scott saw nothing happening from the California Militia That was when he gave the order for the Texicans to start firing and show no mercy.

The Texican Militia was seven hundred twenty three strong but the California Militia combined with the MS-13 gang were six hundred fifteen strong. But this time the Texicans had all seasoned fighters whereas the California Militia had a bunch of kids that probably did not know what a rifle was.

All of the Texicans started firing at onetime causing it to

sound like an explosion went off that was fallowed by hundreds of pops. About one hundred of those at the blockade and behind it fell to their death. As the area at and behind the blockade rained with lead more and more of the young people that had joined Major Morris' movement fell to the ground wounded or dead.

Only a few hundred rounds were fired from behind the blockade but even that stopped as the Texican Militia continued to move forward. By time they reached the blockade only a few of the older California Militia members were still firing their rifles and they were silenced in no time. Hundreds of teens from the age of thirteen up to eighteen were hiding in the shadows crying.

These young people looked for an answer to the chaos around them and only became a part of it. Instead of becoming a part of the answer they became a part of the problem.

The Texican Militia moved through Madisonville arresting every member of the California Militia that they could find. They were easy to find as they were the ones still firing at the Texicans. Most were killed over the next two days of searching the city but theatricals captured forty two of them and four members of the MS-13 gang. All of this took three days.

By this time the Texican Militia had already set up camp in the same parking lot that the California Militia were in. Everything that the California Militia owned the Texicans now owned. The Texicans now had two Humvees and four trucks loaded with supplies.

The young people that had joined this new movement and cult were told to go home although many of them wanted to join the Texican Militia. A trial was held for the California Militia and MS-13 gang members with Scott as the judge. All forty six of them were found guilty of murder among other things. All were given the death penalty. Major David Morris would be executed last. He would be forced to watch while all of his militia was put to death. Only then would he get his punishment.

The sentences were carried out the next morning. Each

person was stood against the outside wall of the Walmart five at a time. Those that resisted were simply shot on sight and their deaths were not clean deaths. When Morris was stood against the wall alone Scott took the rifle to do the job himself.

"You have any last words?" Scott asked Major Morris.

"Yes." Morris answered but Scott interrupted.

"To bad." Scott said as he whipped up the rifle and fired. One shot to the chest pierced Morris' heart. He slowly sunk down to his knees and then fell over. The city of Madisonville volunteered to bury them all in a mass grave which would be marked in some way to commemorate the survival of the city and the help of the Texican Militia.

The day after the executions a man approached Scott with a message. "I've been trying to find you for almost two weeks Sir." the man said. "You are Major Staninski aren't you?"

"Yes I am." Scott admitted.

"Central Command needs to talk with you Sir." the man told Scott. "You'll need to bring at least one truck with you so you can bring back supplies."

With the help of the young man Scott made plans to leave the next morning. Then the young man left to let Central Command know that Major Staninski was on his way.

Scott asked Captain James and three of his men to come with him. They would be taking the ambulance to haul back any supplies given to them. Scott, Evie, and James would ride in the Humvee. Captain Bowers of Company A in charge of the Texicans until they returned.

The next morning Scott and the others left Madisonville and headed straight up Interstate 45 and into Dallas. Three and a half hours after leaving Madisonville they pulled into Central Command. James and his two men stayed with the truck and Humvee while Scott and Evie were taken to an office.

A few minutes later Colonel Hick Melon walked in. He was an older man with gray hair and a gray mustache and beard. He shook Scott's and Evie's hands and then sat in the big chair behind the desk.

With a big smile on his face the Colonel said; "You may not know it but you're a legend in your own time."

Not being a patent man Scott got right down to business. "Why are we here Sir?"

"Oh that's simple." the Colonel said. "Right now I am in charge of all militias in our Republic of Texas; all National Guardsmen, and all other forces. I need you to take over all militias in the Republic of Texas."

Scott and Evie talked with the Colonel for over an hour as Scott wrestled with the idea. By the end of the day he still had not made up his mind. The five of them were put up for the night and ate supper with the Colonel that night. The Colonel had set up a small celebration for Scott hoping that it might sway him to take the position. If he did he would be moved up in rank to General.

After eating and shaking hands Scott and Evie went back to their room where they talk the position over.

"You would have an office. We wouldn't have to freeze in the winter anymore or worry about getting sick in the freezing rain." Evie tried to convince him.

"But I'm not one for an office." Scott said. "I belong out in the field ... doing the fighting and killing the bad guys that do not want us to be a free Republic." Then he looked at Evie and asked; "What about you Babe?"

"I would love to start taking it easy." Evie admitted. "But my place is at your side no matter what you do."

Scott stepped outside to think things over; alone. He looked up at the cool but clear night. The wind was blowing with a cold front coming in. In an hour or so clouds would cover the sky and it would start to rain. Then it would get colder. As he looked up into the sky he thought.

What should I do Father?" Scott asked God's help. *"Evie wants to stay here and live the better life. I ... think ... I want to go back to the Texicans. I'm still young... to young to be locked up in an office. What do you want me to do?"*

Scott thought about it more and more until it started getting cold. He had been so deep in thought that he did not realize that he was standing out in the cold rain. As he turned to go backing he thought came to him; *I need you to free Texas.* Scott then knew what to do.

Scott walked back into the room where Evie was already in bed. She propped herself up on her elbow and asked; "We're going back aren't we?"

As Scott climbed into bed Evie wrapped her arms around her man and said; "I'll be where ever you are." Then she gave him a kiss and added; I like camping anyway and … as long as I have you to keep me warm on all of those cold winter nights …"

Chapter 10

Lone Hunter

The next morning Scott and Evie got up and the five were taken to where a very nice breakfast was waiting for them. With plenty of food on the table they all ate their fill. As they ate Colonel Melon came into the room and got him a plate of food. Then he sat down with the others.

"Made your decision yet?" Melon asked.

"Yes Sir and I'm afraid you're not going to like it." Scott said.

"Before you give me your answer keep in mind that we also have another position for you if you don't want this one." Colonel Melon mentioned.

Scott looked at Evie and then back at Melon. "What position would that be?"

"You would be the judge over any prisoners brought in here." Melon said. "Anyone fighting against our Texas National Guard, militias, or anyone else trying to defend the republic would face you. Your word would be final."

Scott looked back a Evie. "I know what you want Babe."

Before Scott could say another word Evie interrupted him. "I want you to be happy. I want you to do what you want."

Scott looked down as he considered what he wanted to do. Then he finally made his decision. "I'm sorry Sir but I have a militia waiting for me." He turned and walked to the door with Evie behind him. At the door he stopped and looked at Melon. "Out there no one tells me what to do. As your judge or militia leader there would always be someone telling me how to do my job. Maybe when I get older I'll consider one of these jobs but ... for now... I am still young and I have work out there to do."

"Very well Major but these two jobs will not be open very

long." Melon said.

"Yes Sir." Scott said as he walked out of the office.

Before closing the office door Evie turned and said to Melon. You need him out there more than you need him here and you know it."

When Evie closed the door the Colonel sat in his chair wondering what he was going to do. Scott would have been a great head of the militias or even a great judge but, maybe Evie was right. As leader of the Texican Militia he was much more than just great. He was a vicious savage and that was what the Republic of Texas needed.

Scott and Evie met James downstairs. He took them to the truck and Humvee which had both been loaded with more gear than Scot thought that they would get. On top of all of that gear a trailer was attached to the Humvee which was also loaded with gear.

"What all did we get this time?" Scott asked James.

"A lot more food, ammunition, and grenades and ... on the trailer we had LAWs rockets and launchers and claymores ... and a little more food. On the trailer the food is in the form of smoked pork and venison. There is also over one thousand pounds of jerky."

Scott went to the trailer and opened a container of the jerky and pulled one stick out. After taking a bit of the jerky he agreed that it was jerky and then climbed into the Humvee. Evie climbed into the back and James drove. The other two Texicans were in the truck. They drove out of the compound and were heading south in minutes.

Just over three hours later the Humvee came to a stop. Ahead of them was where the Texicans were but Scott could only see hundreds of bodies laying on the interstate and in the ditches.

"Lock-n-load." Scott told the others. "Something is wrong."

Scott pulled up slowly with the other two Texicans in the other truck behind him. Finally they had to stop to keep from driving over dead bodies. Everyone got out of the truck and Humvee and stood ready to fight. However; a fight was not to come. Who ever did this was long gone.

As Scott and the others walked around Scott noticed that many of the dead Texicans looked like that had been lined up and executed. Some of the people of Madisonville came out and talked with Scott. They said that a large amount of Mexican soldiers came up from Huntsville on the interstate. They attacked the Texicans two nights earlier. That was the night that Scott and the others left for Dallas.

Even with the help of the people of Madisonville it took six days to bury all of the dead. A man donated one of his fields as the cemetery. On the fifth night a man came into Scott's camp to talk. The first thing that Scott noticed about the man was the rifle he was carrying.

"May I see your rifle?" Scott asked he man.

The man handed the rifle over to Scott and then Scott recognized it to be his 270.

"Where did you get this?" Scott asked he man.

"I found it out there among the dead." the man said. "Why? Is it yours?"

Scott smiled and looked up at the man. "Yes it is. Would you trade for it?"

The man thought for a moment and then said; "No Sir." Then he handed the 270 over to Scott. "It's yours. I'll go out there and get me another one ... maybe an M-16."

"Thank you young man." Scott said. "This rifle means more to me than most anything."

The young man left and came back later with seven full boxes of 270 ammunition. Scott now had just over one hundred forty rounds for his rifle. He handed his M-16 over to the young man.

"It's a good rifle and has done every well." Scott said.

The man smiled and said; "Thank you Sir.

Then the young man told Scott which direction the Mexican soldiers went. He knew that Scott was going after them. The Mexicans had gone north to Centerville and then turned left on Highway 7. Scott had no idea what he was going to do against what sounded like another Mexican Brigade. Going back to Dallas sounded better by the minute.

That night Scott spent most of his time cleaning and oiling the 270. When he went to bed Evie was already there. She tried to ease his mind but that was not happening. He blamed the death of the Texicans on his not being there. Against a brigade of enemy soldiers he and Evie would have been killed as well.

Scott and the others left Madisonville and drove to Centerville. Then they turned left on Highway 7 and drove towards Robbins and Marquez. Suddenly an explosion stopped the big truck will the supplies.

James whipped the Humvee around to face the truck which slowly drove off into the ditch. With the cab of the truck engulfed in flames the two Texicans had to be dead. Being only about fifty yards from the truck Scott, Evie, and James got out of the Humvee and quickly ran into the woods.

As they ran someone started shooting at them. Once in the cover of the trees and bushes Scott turned around and looked he saw that James had been hit and was laying in the middle of the highway. He could not see Evie who had run into the trees about twenty feet from him. Then he saw almost ten people running across the highway towards them.

"Run Evie." Scott yelled. "Keep running deeper into the woods and I'll find you later." He had no idea if she heard him but he had to run as well.

Shots were being fired wildly into the trees and bushes. After a few minutes one of those rounds found the back of Scott's head in a glancing blow. Trying to hang on Scott move only for another round to knock him out.

When Scott woke up it was morning of the next day. He had been hit twice in the head but, luckily they were both glancing shots. He got to his knees and looked around. Hearing nothing and seeing no movement he slowly stood. Then he slowly worked his way back to the highway.

As Scott looked out of the trees he noticed that the Humvee and trailer were gone. The truck's cab had been to badly burned leaving the truck un-drivable. Then he saw something he hoped he would never see. A little farther up the highway just before entering the trees he saw Evie laying in a pool of blood. He rushed over to her but he was to late. She had been cut down just before she got to the trees.

Scott broke down crying. For a long while he just cried and then suddenly stopped. Like running into a wall his emotions turned from sorrow to anger. He stood and looked around. As if everything was running in slow motion he went down to the truck and got a shovel.

Scott finally realized that he had been in love with Evie. He did not know it until he saw her bloody body laying in that pool of blood. He buried James and Evie there on the side of the highway and then just stood there for a long time. From time to time families would walk by but he just watched them. He looked like a rabid dog ready to pounce on anyone so, no one said anything to him. They just kept walking.

It was easy to see by the two fresh graves why Scott was no longer in his right mind. He just lost the first woman in his life and he wondered if she might have been pregnant. Now she was gone and he had nothing left or; did he? Now there was no sadness. Hatred and extreme anger filled his heart.

Scott stood and looked down at Evie‘s grave. "I‘ll get‘em Babe." he said. “You know I will.”

Finding the EMP guns no longer mattered. Finding the Mexican Brigade no longer mattered. The only thing Scott had on his now bent and twisted mind was finding those that killed Evie. The problem was that they now had his Humvee and could move much easier than he could walk. But which way did they go? Moving on a hunch Scott started walking towards Robbins.

When Scott reached Robbins he stopped to rest. His head had stopped bleeding long ago but he was weak from loss of so much blood. Unable to think clearly his face and shirt were covered in his blood. He looked more like an animal than human. There was no wonder why no one talked to him.

That night Scott hunkered back into the shadows of the trees and bushes in Robbins. That would become a way of life for him from then on. Seeing Evie dead changed him. He was no longer the man everyone knew so well.

The next morning Scott woke up. There would be no coffee that morning. Evie would not be sitting beside him by a campfire. The more he thought about her the more the anger turned to rage. However; he could not allow the rage to keep him from thinking. He did not want to loose the rage in him but every move he made had to be planned.

As Scott looked around he saw nothing that told him which way the truck went. Then he noticed tracks of dooly tires on the side of he road. They had turned south towards Flynn. As Scott passed other people he noticed that they stuck to the far side of the road. They stared at him and looked very scared of him. It was something that he had never seen before. People were always happy to see him. People always smiled when he came around. Only his enemies had a reason to be afraid of him.

By time Scott was about five miles out of Robbins he sat down on the side of he road. He was tired again. Then he realized that he was laying in the tire tracks of a dooly truck. He stood and looked down a driveway that was hard to see but saw nothing ahead. Slowly he started walking up the driveway with his trusty 270 rifle in hand.

The driveway looked more like an animal trail than a driveway. It had been a driveway or small road at onetime but was now grown over. After walking about two hundred yards Scott stopped. Far ahead of him was the Humvee and trailer. He got closer for a better look but stayed in the bushes so he would not be seen.

The Humvee and trailer had been taken to a small cabin. A few men and women were unloading the trailer of the jerky that was in it. Scott wanted so much to take a shot and kill one of them but he knew that he needed to scout out the area first.

Sun Tzu teaches to choose your battlefield. In this case the battlefield had already been chosen but he needed to know the battlefield. He needed to scout out the area and learn the layout of the area around the cabin. This would best be done while the enemy did not know he was there. Taking the first shot then and there would jeopardize that chance to learn the area. With the dark of the night coming Scott slid off a ways from the cabin and sat against a large oak tree. From there he could hear most of the conversations that went on in the cabin that night.

During the first part of the night Scott slid closer to one window so he could hear what all was being said. As he listened one of the men walked outside chewing on some of the jerky. Scott slid close to the cabin and between the many bushes on the side of the cabin. The man walked around coming within just a foot of stepping on Scott but never saw him. Finally the man went back inside when one of the women called him.

Scott then slowly crawled to the trailer. Looking inside he could see much of the jerky was still there so he grabbed some of it. He had not eaten in two days and was hungry. Then he went back to his oak tree and feasted on the hand full of jerky.

Scott was chewing away at the jerky when he remembered that he had seen a wooden crate with the word GRENADES stenciled on it. *Start thinking.* he thought to himself. Two grenades would be enough to takeout the small cabin and everyone in it. He would finish eating first. Then when everyone went to bed he would go back to the trailer and grab some of the grenades.

As Scott looked on and listened to those in the cabin talk he learned that one man and woman seemed to be in charge. One of the men seemed to be married to the second woman. The other five were all men. This was probably a family just trying to survive the hell that Texas had become. He understood their trying to survive but there was no excuse for killing his Evie. As he waited for those in the cabin to fall asleep he himself fell asleep.

Scott woke up a few hours later with mosquito biting his nose. He looked around the large oak and saw no movement and heard no one talking. Leaving his rifle behind he pulled his knife and started crawling towards the trailer.

A few minutes later Scott crawled up beside the trailer. Looking back at the cabin he stood. Then he looked just two fee away and saw one of the men standing there. The man's back was to Scott so he grabbed the man's chin and quickly twisted it while he stabbed the man a few times in the back. A final slice along the throat finished he job. The man fell to the ground.

Plans do not always workout. Scott still had not scouted out the area around the cabin. He had not made any plan of attack and he had already killed one of the enemy. Surely someone would discover the dead man in the morning. Finding a canvas bag in the trailer he tossed seven of the grenades in it along with a litle more of he jerky.

Scott wondered if he should make his stand there or from the side. He could toss a few grenades in the side window or in the now open door. The worse thing was that his rifle was over fifty yards away. *Then again; who needs a rifle when you have a crate of grenades?* he thought to himself.

Being only fifteen feet from the door of the cabin Scott decided to make his stand with the grenades. After pulling the pins on three of the grenades he held the hammers until he was ready. After stepping closer to the cabin door he took one grenade at a time and allowed the hammers to fly off as he threw them into the cabin. Seconds later all three grenades went off almost completely destroying the cabin. Ever time Scott saw someone move in the now burning cabin he pulled the pin on another grenade and tossed it into the cabin. After using nine grenades there was finally no more movement in the fully engulfed cabin.

Scott quickly moved the Humvee and trailer away from the heat of the burning cabin. Then he went back into the woods and got his 270 rifle. On his way back to the Humvee he found an M-16 laying on the ground. It looked like the man he killed with his knife had the M-16 leaning against the trailer. The man also had two extra thirty round magazines on him so Scott took them. After taking a large drink from his canteen he refilled it from the outside well and then go in the Humvee. After another bite from some jerky in his hand he drove out onto the road.

Scott drove back to the truck to load up as much more as he could before others stripped it clean. By time he got to the truck it was daylight. Instantly he jumped out of he Humvee and ordered others in the truck to move.

"This is my truck." he yelled. "Now back off."

"Why should we?" a man yelled back at Scott.

"Because I'll kill you if you don't." Scott said with a firm voice. Then he added; "After I fill this trailer then I will leave and you can have what's left."

The man thought for a moment and then slowly raised his arms. Then he and his friends stepped back away from the truck. Then the man with his hands in the air said that he thought he knew Scott.

"You're ... you're Major Staninski aren't you?" the man asked. "You're the head of the Texican Militia."

"Not anymore." Scott advised the man as he carried things from the truck to the trailer.

The man looked puzzled. "What do you mean?"

Scott stopped and turned to the man. While I was in in Dallas another Mexican Brigade came through and wiped out my militia." He pointed at Evie's grave. "The love of my life is buried over there in one of those graves. I have nothing but anger now."

"You have six new soldiers right here if you want us." the man advised.

Scott stopped and looked at the man. "How old are you?" he asked.

"I'm twenty one Sir. These are my brothers and friends and we have no home ... no place to go anyway."

Scott looked at the youngest one of the six. "How old are you?" he asked.

"I'm fifteen Sir and I can outshoot you any day." the boy said.

Scott smiled and said; "You know ... I bet you could." He looked the young men over and thought for a moment. "Okay then you're all in but here is what I need to do. I need to take two of you with me to Central Command in Dallas for being re-supplied. I'll try to comeback with another truck. If the four of you can hold onto this truck until I get back then we can load everything from this truck into it."

"Is that our first orders Sir?" the oldest young man asked.

"Yes. You're the oldest so I am making you my Lieutenant. You and three others will watch over this truck until I get back. I still need two strong men to go with me to help load the new truck with supplies from Central Command."

Scott found more M-16s in the truck as well as plenty of magazines and ammunition. The young man that he made a Lieutenant was named Josh Waters. The tow going to Dallas with him were Michael Jones and Dan Johnson; both eighteen years old.

Not sure if the four boys could hold onto the truck Scott did not want to leave the trailer. Then again he would becoming back with at least one truck and more supplies in it so he did drop the trailer. Before leaving Scott stepped over to Evie's grave. After a few minutes he climbed back into the humvee and got ready to drive off.

"Lieutenant." Scott said. "Do what ever you have to do to survive and protect this truck and trailer."

"Yes Sir." Lieutenant Waters said as he snapped to and gave a salute.

"We are a militia Lieutenant." Scott advised. "At least in this militia we don't salute."

"Yes Sir." Waters said.

"We should be back tomorrow but the next day at the latest." Scott advised his new Lieutenant. Then he drove off wondering if the truck and trailer would still be there when they got back.

Just over three hours later Scott drove into Central Command. It looked like that had been attacked. The front gate had been hot by some explosives and part of he front door to the building was also hit. Scott had the tow young men stay with the Humvee while he went upstairs to talk to Colonel Melon.

As soon as Scott walked into Melon's office the Colonel stood and asked; “Back so soon?”

Scott gave his report of all that had happened. He told the Colonel about Evie being killed and his revenge he took on them and even about his new young Texicans. When he finished the Colonel just sat there for a moment.

“Man you’ve been through hell since you left here.” the Colonel said. That head of the militias position is still open.”

“No thank you Sir and no head of all militias is going to tell me what to do anyway.”

“I have to have control Major.” the Colonel advised. I can’t have my militias wondering around and not being where I need them. That‘s how that Mexican Brigade got way up here.”

“Oh this is where they came to.” Scott said. “Why don’t you just have one militia that just went from enemy to enemy and wipe them out. That’s what we have been doing and it’s worked so far.”

Colonel Melon just sat in his chair and looked at Scott. “The President is coming down on my backside about this. He wants me to gain control over all fighting forces in this republic.”

“No one controls me Sir.” Scott said.

“Damn it Major.” the Colonel yelled as he quickly stood. “You’re not a militia leader anymore. You’ve become … something else … a vigilante.”

Scott remained quiet in his chair. He had not realized it until then but ever since Evie’s death had was no longer the same man. The Colonel was right. He was no longer the man he used to be. He really was something else now. Then he started to wonder what he should do. Should he tell the young men that just joined him that he was going at it alone from then on? Should he even go at it alone? If he did then Central Command would no longer supply him. Where would he get his ammunition and food?

“Are you listening to me Major?” the Colonel yelled snapping Scott back.

“Yes Sir.” he said.

“Then tell me what you’re going to do.” Colonel Melon insisted. “I need you out there as the leader of the Texican

Militia. You're good at it. You're … El Diablo."

The name given to him by thousands of Mexicans from fear snapped Scott's mind. "That's right." he said to himself but loud enough for the Colonel to hear. "I am El Diablo."

"So tell me. What is El Diablo going to do?" the Colonel asked.

Scott thought for a moment. He knew that the Colonel was right. He had to; El Diablo had to get back out there. The Republic of Texas was falling and it needed him. It needed El Diablo. Scott stood and looked Colonel right in the eye.

"I need two things Sir." he said.

"And what's that?" the Colonel asked.

"I need more soldiers." he said.

"You said you needed two things." the Colonel reminded him.

With a smile Scott added; "I need some red die."

Chapter 11

To Grow Again

Scott left the Colonel's office assured that he would get his soldiers. The Colonel told him that the republic had a three week training camp; a boot camp and there were about seven hundred headwomen almost ready to graduate. He had to wait a week so he would go back and get the other four at the truck. Then he and the young men would come back to get the soldiers.

Scott went down to his Humvee. Looking at both of his new men he asked; "Can you two drive?"

"My father was a truck driver before the war. I have driven big trucks a few times." Michael said.

"Then you'll be driving the dooly ... Sergeant." Then he looked at the other young man also only eighteen years old. "Can you drive my Humvee?"

"Yes Sir." Dan said. "I drove part of the way here."

"That's right. You did." Scott said. "You're my driver."

Scott took Michael around to get one of the trucks. The Colonel already had one waiting for him. Michael climbed up into the driver's seat and cranked it up. Scott signed the paperwork for the truck and went back to the Humvee. Dan was in the driver's seat waiting. When Michael drove the dooly up to the Humvee Scott took the lead and they were off.

Three and a half hours later Scott pulled up to the burned truck. Two of the young men came out of the truck happy to see them.

"Where's the other two?" Scott asked.

"They're dead Sir." Lieutenant Waters said. "Some men came by and laughed at us trying to protect your truck. They forced their way by us and started to take things. We raised out rifles and they started firing at us. When it was over Teddy and

Sam were dead."

"What about the men that attacked you?" Scott asked.

"Oh they're dead Sir." the Lieutenant said with a big smile. "We protected your truck but it cost us two men."

"You young men need to get used to that." Scott said. "We had an evil communist president that gave Texas back to Mexico. Now we have Mexicans coming into our Republic of Texas trying to take it. We will loose men from time to time. That is the cost of a free republic."

After everything was moved from the burned truck to the good dooly truck Scot climbed into his Humvee. The others climbed in the back of the dooly and they were off. On their way to Dallas they ran into a bad storm causing them to not get into Central Command until after dark. They had to sleep in the truck and Humvee that night.

The next morning Scott went up to see Colonel Melon. As he walked into the office he saw many others in there talking with Melon. Major Layton of the Layton Militia was there as well as General Bolton and other militia leaders all wanting their cut of the soldiers that were about to graduate from the training camp. Scott just stood there holding the door knob.

Melon stood and said; "Come on in Major." he said.

"Major." Layton said. "What is he a major of?"

Scot got mad and quickly stepped up to Layton. "Over one thousand soldiers that gave their lives for this republic."

"Yes ... you got them all killed." Layton said as he laughed.

Scott jumped at Layton but others grabbed him and held him back.

"Gentlemen." Melon yelled. "Stop it."

"He even got his woman killed." Layton just had to say.

Scott lunged at Layton again but was still being held back.

"Shut up Layton or I'll let him have you." Melon yelled. Then he looked into Layton's eyes and added; "And he'll kill you."

Everyone gained their composure and the meeting went on. There were one hundred ninety eight. Soldiers that would be graduating the next day and four militia leaders stood in Melon's office wanting them. By the end of the day the Texican Militia got only one hundred of them. The other ninety eight of them were going to the other militias.

During the rest of the day the four militia leaders were told how and what the soldiers were being taught. Some of them had been trained in using explosives; most in just fighting techniques and a few were trained in being snipers. After the meeting Scott tried to talk to Melon alone but the other leaders had the same thing mind.

Out of desperation Scott grabbed Melon's head and pulled his ear close. Then he whispered; "I want those snipers."

"Let the Colonel go." Layton yelled as he started to grab Scott.

Go ahead Lipton." he said mocking Layton's name. '"You just think about touching me and I'll kill you ... you fagit son of a whore."

"What is it with you two?" Bolton asked.

"He's a fagit ... a queer ... an abomination in the eyes of God." Scott said. "And after that remark about Evie ... a dead man. Your body just doesn't know it yet."

It was not just Layton being gay that bothered Scott. He and others had heard what he did with some of his younger soldiers. There was also that something in the back of Scott's mind that he did not like about Layton. There was just something about Layton that Scott did not like other than his being gay.

Scott left the meeting and went back to the others. They moved their vehicles to an empty field close by and set up camp. "We're only getting one hundred of he soldiers tomorrow." he told the others. "Lieutenant. You will be in charge of anyone we get under the age of ... lets say under nineteen. It will be your job to get them ready to fight."

That night Scott stepped out into the field to pray.

"I don't understand what you are doing Father. I puttyroots in you and then I lost everything. I lost Evie. I lost my entire militia

Lord. What am I doing wrong?" Scott asked God.

Then the words came to his mind. *I am the same yesterday, today, and tomorrow. If I have helped you yesterday then why should I not help you today or tomorrow?*

"Then why did you take Evie from me?" Scott asked God.

Others took her from you but do not worry. I will send you someone that will lift you up. She will be your backbone and your source of power. She will be your friend first and then you will know her.

Scott walked back into camp almost more confused that when he left. As he sat by the campfire others came to Scott wanting to join the Texican Militia. Word got out that The Texicans were in Dallas and they came in droves wanting to join. The other militias in the field next to the Texicans watched not believing what they were seeing. How could so many people want to join the Texicans and not them?

Three days had passed by time the one hundred soldiers were released to Scott who already two hundred twenty four soldiers in camp. That morning he gave everyone in the camp a speech.

"About one hundred of you are from the training camp. The other ... over two hundred are no different. You will fight and you will obey orders ... or I will have you shot. Now show me hands of how many of you need tents."

Scott tried to count the tents but some of the volunteers also needed winter clothing and firearms. He put Peg Nelson in charge of the group until he returned. She was the head of the class out of the one hundred trainees.

By the way Nelson." Scott looked back and said; "You're my first Captain. Good job in the Training Camp."

Scott left to talk with Melon again. He knocked on the door and the Colonel called him in.

"Oh Major." Melon said. "What can I do you for ... again?"

I have over two hundred that joined my militia since saw you the other day." Scott advised Melon.

"Yes I know. I have been watching your camp grow out

there." Melon said ever so proud of Scott. "So why afe you here?"

"I need additional things now." Scott said not planning to stop with his request. "I need two hundred tents, one hundred M-16s and about half a truck of ammunition ... oh and two more trucks."

"Did you know ... Major ... that all of these things are donated to us from other states in the United States. Ninety percent of the ammunition comes from Arkansas."

"Yes Sir I know and we still need some of that." Scott insisted.

Colonel Melon looked at this man standing in front of him that had already done more damage to the Mexicans than all of the other militias put together. He took in a deep breath and let it out. Then he got on the radio and called the warehouse.

He ordered three more trucks to be loaded with two hundred tents, one hundred M-16s, forty crates of ammunition and one truck was to be loaded with just MREs. Then he called he lieutenant in charge with loading the trucks to his office. A few minutes later the lieutenant came in the office and snapped to attention in front of the Colonel.

"Lieutenant ... how often do any of these trucks just ... oh ... lets say just come up missing?"

"Not one Sir since I took over Sir." the young female lieutenant said.

"Oh my God." Scott said as he looked at the Lieutenant.

"What's wrong Major?' the Colonel asked.

"The Lieutenant." Scott said. "She looks just like ..." he stopped before saying that she looked like Evie. "Nothing Sir."

"Back to you Lieutenant." the Colonel said. "You're about to loose your first trucks."

The Lieutenant looked at the Colonel. "I'm what Sir?"

"The Major here is going on a secret mission and I do not need any paperwork on it." he told her. "Do you understand Lieutenant?"

The Lieutenant took in a deep breath and then said; "Yes

Sir."

"Don't worry Lieutenant. I'll cover your ass on this."

"But Sir." the Lieutenant asked. "If I was not here to be questioned then it might be easier to … loose these things."

"What do you mean?" the Colonel asked.

"I have always wanted to be apart of the Texican Militia. If I was to be transferred … if I was not here …"

"Major?" the Colonel asked Scott. "Can you use her?"

"Sir." she said. "I would like to add that I am a trained and excellent sniper."

Scott cheered up. "Yes Sir. I can use another sniper for an idea I have."

"Lieutenant. You are being transferred to the Texican Militia with no paperwork. Get all your gear together and meet the Major before he has to leave. And say nothing to anyone. You are under special orders."

"Thank you Sir." the Lieutenant said. Then she realized that she answered wrong. "I mean yes Sir."

"Both of you … get out of here."

As Scott and the Lieutenant walked out of the office he told her that they were over in the field.

"Oh I know Sir. I've been watching you … I mean all of you."

As the Lieutenant ran off to get her gear he passed General Bolton. The shook hands and talked over old times in Afghanistan.

"I'm proud of you boy." Bolton told Scott. "You've come along ways."

When Scott left he hallway Bolton stepped over to Melon's office. Melon was still at his door watching Scott walk away.

"He's a good man Colonel." Bolton said. "If only one man frees the Republic of Texas it will be Major Staninski there.

"Yeah I know." Melon said.

"So is that why you gave him the free trucks and supplies?"

Melon quickly looked at Bolton. "You heard us talking?"

"I could hear you two all the way down the hall but don't

worry. No one else was around."

The two men went back inside the office and this time shut the door. Then they toasted a glass of Brandy to Scot; to El Diablo.

Scott walked back out to the camp. He thought about getting everyone ready to move out but he had no idea as to which way to go. Then eighteen year old Dan asked Scott why he did not just stay there for a few more days.

You have all of these people coming here to join you and then you won't be here for them. You need soldiers and they are coming in every day." Dan Said. "I know I'm out of place here Sir but why leave with all of these people coming in?"

Scott smiled. "Out of the mouths of Babes." He put his hand on Dan's shoulder and added; "You're right Young man. I think we need and have deserved a rest of ... oh let's say a few days?"

Scott sent out word throughout the Texicans that they would be staying for at least three days. Then he sat back in his folding chair and added; "Oh that feels good."

A few minutes later Lieutenant Bailey showed up with her gear. She lay her things close to Scott and then told him that she had no tent. He told her to get one out of he truck. She did and set it up beside Scott's tent. Then she came back to the campfire and unfolded a chair of her own and placed it close to Scott. After getting a cup of coffee she sat down and listened to what was being said.

Scott sent Peg to Colonel Melon's office with a message. When she got to the Colonel's office she knocked and entered with permission. She stepped up to the desk and snapped to with a salute.

"This is one of his brats." Layton said. He was there to complain about the Texicans still hanging around. The truth was that he was angry about no getting any of the new people coming in. They were all joining the Texicans.

"What's wrong Layton?" Lieutenant Nelson said. "Could you be upset that I'm not a young boy that you can ... talk to?"

"I ought to slap you for that." Layton said.

“You get close enough and I’ll slit your throat.” she responded.

The Colonel was having fun listening to them but he had work to do. “May I help you.”

“I’m Lieutenant Nelson of the Texicans Sir. Major Staninski sends his respects and two requests Sir.”

“Now I can see that this lady has had some training. You see how she first said that her Major sends his respects. Perfect lead off.” he complimented her. “You have my attention Lieutenant. What two things does he need?”

“Major Staninski needs orders and his ... red die you promised him Sir.” she said sharply.

“What’s he doing right now?” Melon asked.

“The Texicans are sitting still out there for now. With so many people coming in to join us it seems to be a shame to leave so quickly Sir.”

“Lieutenant.” the colonel said. “Please tell the Major that I will send him orders in ... oh lets say a few days. In the meantime recruit as many as he can and then I need to see him before he leaves.”

“Yes Sir.” the Lieutenant said.

“Dismissed.”

Lieutenant Nelson gave a solute and then left the office. Colonel Melon stood and smiled. “Now that’s an officer.”

Nelson returned to Scott and told him what Melon said. He was happy to be allowed to stay and continue to recruit for the Texican Militia. However; this was causing problems with the other militia leaders. Very few of the people coming into Dallas wanted to join them. Almost all of them wanted to join the Texicans.

Layton continued to cause problems for Scott including telling lies about him and the Texicans. He told people that Scott got all of his people killed including his girlfriend. Then one day he came into Scott’s camp to start trouble face-to-face.

“Major.” Layton yelled as he walked into the camp. “I want to talk to you.”

Still sitting in his chair Scott said; “I fixing to kill you Lipton.” he said still making fun of Layton’s last name.

“Stand when I talk to you.” Layton yelled.

“You’re a Major just like me Dumb Ass” Scott said with a smile. Even if you were my superior I have no respect for you at all.”

“I just excepted the position of Head of Militias.” Layton advised. “I am your superior now.”

“Good. Now you can molest even more young men. Even if you did take that job I am on a special mission and you have nothing to do with me.” Scott insisted.

Layton got mad and kicked Scott’s chair so hard it broke causing him to fall on the ground. Instantly Scott jumped up and hit Layton as hard as he could almost knocking him out.

“Get out of my camp you son of a whore. If you come back I will shoot you on sight.”

“I’ll be back.” Layton said as he stormed out of the camp. Scott had no idea as to what Layton would do but he was sure that Layton was not through with him. About an hour later a messenger came and told Scott that Colonel Melon wanted to see him.

Scott checked his pistol. *Loaded and chambered.* He was going to end this now. When he walked into the Colonel’s office he was surprised to see no one else in he office except the Colonel.

“Got a mission for your Texicans.” the Colonel said. Then he went on to give Scott the details and a few maps that might help.

Suddenly Layton came into the office not knowing that Scott was there. “You.”

“No … me.” Scott said.

“This man struck me earlier.” Layton said. Then he looked at Scott and added; ”You’re under arrest.”

Then Layton lunged at Scott to grab him Scott pulled his pistol and quickly fired just grazing Layton’s neck.

With Layton laying on the floor at one side of the room the Colonel yelled and ordered Scott to holster his pistol. Then he calmly gave Scott his orders as if noting had happened.

“You’re under arrest.” Layton yelled as soon as he was back upon his feet.

“Shut up Layton or I’ll shoot you myself.” Colonel Melon said. “I wish he had killed you. I’m tired of you myself.”

Layton stormed out of the room holding a rag against his neck. Then Melon looked at Scott and said; “I didn’t really mean that you know.”

“Yes Sir.” Scott said.

“He really will be good in that job.” the Colonel added.

“Yes Sir.” Scott replied again.

The Colonel continued to tell Scott who he was going after and where they were. Then Scott left and went back to camp. He gave orders to break camp the next morning. He asked Peg how many they had at that time. She smiled and said that the Texicans were five hundred seventeen strong and still growing.

“Okay then.” Scott said to Peg. “By the way. You’re doing a great job.”

“Thank you Sir.” she replied. “Where are we headed tomorrow?”

“That big Mexican Brigade just wiped out one of our militias in west Texas. Now they are heading back in this direction.”

“Any reason they are coming back here?” Peg asked.

“A Brigade General Diego Lopez leads that brigade and he is hunting someone.” Scott said as he packed his backpack.

“Who is he hunting Sir?” Peg asked knowing the answer anyway.

Scott stood and faced her. Then he said; “Me. He’s hunting me.”

Chapter 12

The Bridge

Brigade General Diego Lopez was not actually going after Scott so much as he was going after El Diablo. Just before Scott lead the Texicans out of Dallas a messenger came to Scott.

"This is from Colonel Melon Sir." the young man said as he handed Scott a small bottle of red die.

Scott looked back at the building where Melon's office was and saw the Colonel standing at the big window. He raised he bottle thanking the Colonel. Melon raised his hand and waved back.

The Texicans could only travel as fast as the Texicans could walk. As they traveled Scott and peg worked together to choose other ranks to be used in the militia. Scott wanted four Captains which would have just over the one hundred twenty needed for a company. Those Captains would answer to Peg. Each Captain would organize their company but the ranks they uses had to be approved by Scott himself.

Peg would be useful in this as she knew almost all of the one hundred Texicans that she was in the Training Camp with. Scott would choose his Captains from them. She finally came up with four names and called those four to meet with Scott.

Randy Sales, Paul Polas, Mary Causk, and Vern Divings were called on and met in Scott's camp on the fourth night after leaving Dallas. Lieutenant Josh Waters was also called to this meeting.

First Scott made sure that these people would take the rank and responsibility he gave them. All four excepted the rank of Captain and the responsibility of taking on a company. He made sure that Lieutenant Waters was also a Company commander but with the rank of lieutenant; only because of his age and lack of experience. Anyone under the age of nineteen that joined the Texicans went into his company. The next day they would stay in the large field that they were in and choose which Texicans went into which company.

Lieutenant Waters' Company E of very young people would be used scamp guards at night from then on. They would also be the ones used to guard over things like the trucks and of course; Scott's Humvee. The next day the Texicans continued their march to catch up with the Mexican Brigade.

Being outnumbered almost seven to one the Texicans would not win an all out face to face fight. These Mexican soldiers had already wiped out two Texas militias and anyone else that got in their way so they had plenty of experience in fighting.

Major Layton was in the Colonel's office with Major Bolton when Colonel Melon told them that he had sent the Texican Militia to the area of Marlin to stop Brigade General Diego Lopez. Layton started thinking that if he could be the one to wipe out the Mexican brigade then he would be the hero and not Scott. Taking that from Scott would be the perfect way to get back at him. *Hit me will you.* he thought.

Having so much hate towards Scott, Major Layton decided to take the glory from Scott by moving his militia farther to the west that marlin where Scott would be. In this way he would find the Mexican brigade long before Scott would. Without orders to move out Layton took his militia out of Dallas in the midlife night. He took his 830 strong to the western side of Waco and hen moved south. There his militia sat waiting for Brigade General Lopez a good twenty miles west of where the Texican Militia was.

The next day scouts that Layton had sent out came with news. A large Mexican brigade was moving eastward towards Layton's militia. Lopez had also sent out scouts that had reported to him that El Diablo was waiting for him just west of Waco. Lopez thought that Layton's militia was Scott's Texican Militia.

Layton moved his militia to the east side of a vast field. Spotted patched of trees gave some cover but not much. Layton had his people move into the trees to fight from but he still had over five hundred that had no cover. After a speech to them telling them that this was to be the final battle to free the Republic of Texas they were ready to do anything he wanted.

On the other had Lopez had no cover except a few groups of scattered trees if he could take them from Layton's people. The next morning Layton's militia waiting on the eastern side of he very large clearing and Brigade General Lopez stood on the western side. The clearing was so large that almost a mile stood between the two sides with only a few groups of trees blocking their view. Layton and Lopez could still see the other leader's people.

There was about to be a big fight and Layton was still outnumbered at least four to one but all he had on his mind was taking the glory from Scott. He did not consider being wiped out. After all. He had to be much smarter than Lopez. What Layton did no know was that Lopez had been educated in the best tactics of war that Mexico had to offer.

Suddenly a shot was fired from Layton's militia and the battle was on. Instantly Lopez sent his four thousand soldiers across the field. Layton had his militia open fire. For over an hour the two sides fought. Groups of tree cover were defended, lost, and then regained. After only two hours Lopez had lost over three thousand soldiers but Layton had already lost the fight. Layton and nineteen of his militia kicked some serious butts but still surrendered to Lopez.

Lopez pulled his sword as he walked up to Layton who was on his knees. "El Diablo ... no way." He spoke broken English but well enough to be understood. Then he raised his sword.

"I'm not El Diablo." Layton said as he hoped to get out of there alive.

Lopez slowly lowered his sword. "What do you ... mean?" he asked.

"El Diablo is a few miles to the east waiting for you." the Major turned coward said. "He sent us by force to fight you. Please allow us to leave in peace but don't send us back to him."

Layton pleaded for his life and not the lives of his militiamen and they saw it.

Lopez thought for a moment. “So … you are not El Diablo and he is east of here waiting for me?”

“Yes. He is on the other side of Waco someplace.” Layton said.

“Stand.” Lopez told Layton. “You go tell him that I am coming.”

“All of us may go?” Layton asked.

“No.” Lopez said. “Two will go with you but the others will be executed for their sins against Mexico. Tell El Diablo that I will wait two days and then leave this place.”

Lopez chose two women to go with Layton and then had them leave. As they left they could hear he screams of the others being executed by sword. Their heads had been removed.

That night Layton and the two women with him stopped to rest. As the women slept Layton sneaked off into the night leaving the two women alone. When they woke up the next morning and found that they were alone they decided to continue ahead and find the Texicans. They knew that they would be safe then.

When the women finally reached the Texican Militia they were brought to Scott. The two women were given food and water. Then they told Scott all that they knew including the part about Layton abandoning them the night before. Scott knew that he did not think much of Layton but did not think he was a coward.

By this time the Texicans were five hundred eighty two strong but Lopez still had just under five thousand soldiers. The Texican Militia was outnumbered at least seven to one. When the darkness of the night came Scott left the camp for some privacy.

“Well Father … looks like I did it again. Lopez will be here in a day or so and we are greatly outnumbered. What can we do against so many? Scott walked around some and then continued. *What can I do Father?”*

Scott took a few more steps and then the thought cam to him.

Trust in the Lord.

Scott had no idea what he was going to do but the only weapon that he had was God. Many of the Texicans did not believe in God but they did trust Scott's decisions after he had prayer. As he sat by the campfire deep in thought Lieutenant Bailey sat beside him. He jumped from shock of someone suddenly being beside him.

"Oh I'm sorry Sir." she said making sure she still gave him a cute little smile. "I didn't mean to scare you."

"Oh that's okay Bailey."

"In the colonel's office you said something about me looking like someone." Bailey said. "Who was she?"

Scott took a deep breath and let it out. Then he told Bailey all about Evie. He admitted that he thought that he was in love but he was not sure.

"I'm sorry that you lost her ... Sir." Bailey said.

To change the subject Scot mentioned an idea he had. "I was thinking about forming a company or fire team of just snipers ... sharpshooters that would just pick off enemy officers. Would you like to lead that team?"

"Yes Sir I sure would." Bailey said eager to start.

"Then pick out some of the Texicans that you know shoot well. Melon gave mea few sniper's rifles; M-14 rifles with scopes. They're heavy but 308 calibers are good sniper calibers.

"I know three people that were in the Training Camp with me and they already have their rifles and scopes."

"Good. Bring them tome tomorrow morning." Scott said.

"Yes Sir." Bailey said as she got up and left the campfire.

Scott watched bailey walk away and noticed that even then she looked like Evie. But he did not want to start another relationship. In two days they might all be dead anyway.

Bright and early the next morning Bailey brought her three friends to Scott. They're names were Dale Powers, Gene Powers, and Jane Obern. Dale and gene were twin brothers. Scott stood to talk with them.

"You will be my sniper squad. Lieutenant Bailey here will be your Lieutenant. She will answer directly to me as the Captains do. Dismissed."

Scott sat back down in his chair by the campfire and asked Lieutenant Bailey to have the others in her squad pitch their tents close to his tent. In that way he could give them orders in a second's notice.

Just before noon Scott got word that Lopez and his half of a brigade were just three miles away. He ordered the Texicans to line up on the river bank. He pulled out his bottle of red die and rubbed it all over any exposed skin he had. Now he was ready to fight.

Lopez would have to cross the river to get to them. The river. Had steep banks, a good fifty feet high on both sides. The only way that Lopez could cross quickly would be to storm the bridge which Scott had heavily guarded. The Texicans were spread out for almost one mile on each side of he highway bridge. Scott had his Sniper Team set up to fire across the bridge on his orders.

A few minutes after the Texicans got ready Lopez's forces showed themselves coming up the highway. Then gunfire started coming from the trees on the western side of he river. Texicans on the eastern side of the river had to move back to keep from being wiped out. Unfortunately; this kept them from being able to shoot any Mexican soldiers crossing the river.

Mexican soldiers started dropping down into the river and crossing the river by the hundreds. With none of the Texicans able to get close enough to the river bank to fire down into the river many of the Mexicans had crossed and were climbing the eastern bank. But God had other plans.

Earlier that morning a large thunderstorm broke out many miles to the north. For hours the area was flooded with heavy rain. A lake on the river quickly filled. Workers tried to open the gates but they would not move. Suddenly there was a loud cracking sound and the workers abandoned the dam. Then the dam broke with a force that looked like an explosion. A wall of water fifteen feet high began to move down the river.

By time half of Lopez's soldiers were crossing the river this fifteen foot tall wall of water came through taking out about two hundred of the Mexican soldiers. Scott stood tall knowing that God came through for him yet again.

The Texicans concentrated their fire on the other bank and from time to time shot a Mexican soldier that was able to climb up on their side. The snipers were busy knocking down Mexican officers and other ranks of soldiers far down the highway.

Then the clouds opened up and the sun shined through on one spot of the highway where Scott stood. As the sun highlighted the red colored El Diablo most of the Mexican soldiers stopped firing their rifles. Some even turned and ran. They had heard how that El Diablo had come and destroyed many of their fellow countrymen and taken their souls to Hell. They wanted no part of this and over six hundred deserted Lopez and ran.

Then the clouds closed up and El Diablo vanished. Actually Scott just stepped to the side of he highway but it looked like he vanished. This alone cause another fifty or more to desert Lopez.

Lopez retreated with the few soldiers that he had left. He regrouped about one mile back from the bridge. The Texicans continued to fire on any Mexican soldiers that climbed out of the river. With no one on the other side of he river firing back at them the Texicans moved up to the edge of the river bank. From there they continued to fire on soldiers still climbing the bank and those that were in the water.

After regrouping Lopez counted his soldiers. He only had two hundred twenty three left. There was nothing else to do but maybe head back to Mexico. He still considered drawing the Texicans on that side of he river for another fight.

The Texicans lost twenty seven with another thirty one wounded; thirteen badly wounded. They captured fifty nine of the Mexican soldier all of which Scott had shot for what he called treason against the republic of Texas. He mainly did it because Lopez had executed so many of Layton's people after they surrendered. He did spare one soldier to deliver a message to Lopez.

After the other prisoners were executed the one soldier was brought to Scott. At that time Scott was very busy; sitting in his chair by the campfire sipping on a cup of coffee. Using a Texican as a translator he asked the soldier if he knew who he was.

"El Diablo." the soldier said as he shook.

"I need you to do something for me." Scott said. "Will you help me deliver a message to Lopez?"

The soldier cried and agreed to do what ever El Diablo wanted.

"Tell Lopez that..." he looked at the solder. "... I coming for him ..." Then he stood and stepped closer to the soldier to scare him a bit more. "... and when I catch him I'm going to tear his heart out and eat it. Then I'm going to take his soul to the deepest part of Hell and leave him there for eternity."

The soldier was still crying like a baby. Part of his crying was because he was happy that he was being released. The other reason he was crying was just because he really believed hat he was in the presents of El Diablo; the devil himself.

Scott had the prisoner given food and water and then he was sent across the bridge. After that Scott returned to his chair, campfire, and cup of coffee. He called for his Captains and Lieutenants Bailey and Waters. When they all finally go there he had a talk with them about what he wanted done.

"First I am promoting Lieutenant Bailey and Lieutenant Waters to the rank of Captain. From now on when I call for my Captains ... like right now... you all will come." he told them. Then he went on to say; "I need Texicans on the river bank to watch for any of Lopez's soldiers. I need Company A on the river bank and south side of the bridge. I need Company B on the north side of the bridge. I need Captains Bailey and Waters on the bridge. Bailey ... help train Water's people. They are young and inexperienced."

Scott thought about everything and was wondering how long they might be waiting for an answer from Lopez. Then he added; "In case we are here a few days each day at noon Company A will be replaced by Company C and Company D will replace

Company B. Then at noon the next day you all will swap back again. We might be here a week or so. Dismissed."

It was late in the evening the next day before the same soldier that Scott sent to Lopez returned with a message. Lopez wanted El Diablo to come get him. Scott called Captain Nelson and told her to get the Texicans ready. They would not break camp but they would be moving across the bridge in a day or so.

Scott was thinking about making Lopez have to wait for them to cross the river. On the other hand crossing the next daylight best. There was just no way of knowing what ambushes awaited them on the other side. That night he sent Company D across the river a few people at a time. It would be their job to scout out the area just on the other side of the river.

When the dark of the night came Company D went to the bridge. Four of five at a time crossed the bridge and then took up defenses on the other side while others came across. Captain Divings remained behind to be the last in his company to cross. Then the Captain stayed at the bridge while his Company searched the area for any traps of ambushes.

Scott sat in his camp and listened to the radio so he could hear what all was going on. A few tripwires and booby traps were found but that was all. After moving in a quarter of a mile from the bridge Company D stopped. Not one Mexican soldier had been found.

Scott knew from the report of the two women that the Texicans had Lopez outnumbered almost three to one. But he still did not want to send all of the Texicans over the bridge just to be caught between Lopez's army and the river. Then they would be the ones being shot in the river. The water in the river had gone back down but swimming across it was not an option.

He contacted Captain Divings and told him that he was also sending over Companies B and C. As they crossed they spread out. By morning everyone had crossed except for Scott, Company E and Bailey's snipers. Company E watched the camp and surrounding area while Bailey's snipers set up at the bridge to keep any Mexican soldiers from coming back across.

Companies A and B moved out from the bridge almost a mile and they still found no one. Lopez must have sent word to come get him just to slow down the Texican Militia. It worked. Two companies at a time came back across the river and packed their gear. Then Scott took the lead and moved allof the Texicans across the bridge.

When the Texicans were about two miles west of the bridge they heard a number of massive explosions behind them. Scott stopped everyone and sent Company E to find out what was going on behind them. A few hours later they returned with bad news.

Somehow Lopez got on the eastern side of the river. Scott's Texicans had somehow passed them. But the worse news was that Lopez blew the bridge up. There would be no easy way to cross the river. It would be much easier to go up or down river and cross another bridge. But which direction was the closest bridge? It was time to make another decision. He had a 50/50 chance of choosing the right direction but then he also had a 50/50 chance of choosing the wrong decision. He decided to fallow the highway and turn to the north when they could.

Lopez had fooled Scott and made him look like a fool. This did not set well with Scott or the Texicans under him. A few of the Texicans started turning against Scott. They were all behind him as long as everything was going their way but let one thing go wrong and a few of them turned on him. That night Scott sought help again.

"I'm in trouble again Father. I finally outnumber my enemy but he slipped right by me leaving me no way to catch him. Please guide me Lord. My own people are turning against me. Out of all of the times you helped us to win they finally are defeated and they cannot handle it. Please guide me Lord. The Texicans ... the whole militia is in your hands. I await your answer."

Scott walked back into camp and found three of the Texicans upset with him. He sat in his chair by the fire and waited for their

words. Finally it came.

"Why have you lead us to the north?" one woman said. She semitone the instigator. We have not seen abridge back across the river all day and I doubt if we will see one tomorrow."

"Hold your tongue woman." Captain Sales said. "Sorry Sir. She is in my company. I'll take care of her."

"No!" Scott said. "Let her speak."

Now the woman could think of nothing to say so Scott did. "You think it is easy to lead so many?" He looked at the woman. "You think I am a god that makes no mistakes?" Then he turned and said; "Leave me alone Fool" You can leave if you want but if you stay you will stay away from me." He whipped around and looked at her again. "That's an order."

The woman and her two friends left Scott's camp. Captain Sales fallowed her. He was going to say his peace to them when they got back to their camp.

Scott thought about what the woman had said. She was right about one thing. He had to do something and quick. He already knew of a bridge that they would reach the next day but all of the Texicans already knew about it. He hoped that things would change after they all saw and crossed the bridge.

The next morning the moral in camp was much better. Knowing that they would be crossing the bridge that day had everyone feeling better. Scott was not the only one that wanted to catch up with Lopez. They all did. Knowing that he had to show the bridge as quickly as possible the Texicans broke camp before daylight. By 0900 hours that morning the bridge came into sight.

The bridge was a small one that the owner of the land built many years earlier. It was in bad shape but good enough for a few of the Texicans to cross at a time. By noon all of the Texicans were on the eastern side of the river again. Because Scott was not sure if the bridge would hold the weight of he trucks he had them unloaded and the supplies carried across the bridge. Only then did the empty trucks cross with no problems. The trucks were reloaded and the Texicans were on their way again.

All of the bridges below the broken dam were wiped out so

they had to continue north until they came to the small bridge. Scott knew that they were many miles north of the bridge that Lopez blew up and wondered where Lopez could be. Surely he was heading back to Mexico but, until they got back to the Marlin area he would not find where Lopez went.

It took two days to get back to their old camp between Marlin and the bridge. Scott had the Texicans set up camp again and asked them all to look for signs that would show which direction Lopez went. Then they would fallow him.

Late that evening as Scott sat in his chair by the campfire the woman that had given him trouble a few days earlier came to him again. This time she wanted to apologize for how she acted the other day. When Scot told her that he had already forgiven her she gave him a big hug and then ran off. It was like forgiving her was the best thing that ever happened to her.

As the sun went down Scott felt a tap on his shoulder. It was Lieutenant bailey with an opened MRE just like Evie used to do.

"I noticed that you don't eat much and we need to keep up our strength don't we."

"Thank you Lieutenant." Scott said.

"Just call me Paula when we're off duty ... if you don't mind Sir."

Scott smiled and said; "If you stop calling me Sir."

"May I sit with you ... If I don't call you Sir then what do I call you?"

"My first name is Scott." he advised her.

"Then may I sit with you ... Scott?"

"Of course." he told her.

Chapter 13

Layton's Return

The next morning Scott got word that Lopez had headed into and quickly went through Marlin. The Texicans broke camp and fallowed. Many of the people in Marlin tried to get Scott and his Texicans to stop and talk but they did not have time. Many in the town were offended but when they found out that they were after Lopez they understood.

A few days earlier Lopez and his two hundred twenty three soldiers came through the town taking what ever they wanted. Many of the young women and even girls were raped by his soldiers and anyone that tried to stop them was shot on sight. Thirteen people of the town were killed and another twenty were badly wounded from gunshots and knife cuts and stabs.

Lopez loved executing people by cutting off their heads with his sword. Executing someone was something that a leader was never suppose to do although Scott did it from time to time. That duty is suppose to be passed on to the lower ranks with an officer in charge.

Two days later the Texican Militia walked into the town of Kosse. As usual they were greeted with cheers and gifts of food. The Texicans set up camp for the night and Scott quickly found his way to his folding chair by his campfire. He was not drinking any coffee yet but that was only because it was brewing.

One of he men that lived just north of Kosse a few miles grew his own coffee beans. He knew how much Scott loved his coffee and brought him a gift of about one hundred pounds of coffee beans from the previous year‘s harvest.

“What do I own you for these coffee beans?” Scott asked the old man.

“Only one thing.” the old man said. “Kill that Lopez fellow.

When he came through he came to my farm and just took over seven hundred pounds of coffee from me."

"Oh I don't want the last of your coffee." Scott told him.

"I still have about two hundred pounds of last year's stock that, that Mexican bastard didn't find. Just get him and we're even."

Scott excepted the gift and thanked he man. The coffee could not have come at a better time. The Texicans were almost out of coffee. Scott kept twenty pounds of the coffee beans and had the rest of it passed out to the Texicans. Scott sat back in his chair smiling. He had plenty of coffee and that made him happy.

"You're still not eating Sir." a woman's voice came from Scott's left. It was Paula carrying another MRE for Scott's breakfast. "I've been watching and you have not eaten this morning."

"I'll eat that only if you eat with me." Scott told her.

After handing Scott the warm MRE of bacon and eggs Paula went back to the truck and got her one. Then she returned and sat in a chair beside Scott and ate breakfast with him. Scott was starting to enjoy the time Paula spent with him. She was in so many way just like Evie but not in other ways. Paula was Paula not Evie. She could only be herself. Although he loved Evie he was not in love.

That evening Scott told Captain Nelson that the Texicans would be breaking camp the next morning. He wanted to move out at first light. Nelson told the other Captains and then set back at the campfire with Scott.

"Your starting to like Paula aren't you?" Nelson asked. Only she knew that she also had an interest in Scott.

"I ... guess so. Why?" Scott asked her.

Nelson smiled and added; "Everyone sees it."

"She just looks a lot like Evie and that's all." Scott tried to defend himself.

Oh it's okay Sir." Nelson said. "Everyone likes it. They like seeing you happy again."

The conversation changed to matters at hand like Lopez and

his path of destruction. Was Lopez heading back to Mexico to re-supply of did he have something else in mind?

Scott worried about the Republic of Texas. While Texas was running out of young men to fight for freedom Mexico with Central and South America still had plenty.

That night Scott did not sleep well. He worried a great deal about the future of the republic. He wanted to be an American more but since the American president turned dictator and gave Texas to Mexico he chose to fight for the Republic of Texas.

"Good night ... Major." Paula said from her tnt next to Scott's.

"Good night Captain." Scott replied.

Then someone else a few tents away yelled: "Good night John Boy."

That started everyone that heard it to laughing. Scott smiled and knew that the entire camp must have been listening. But it was funny so he continued to smile until he fell asleep.

Around 0400 hours the camp guard woke Scott up to get ready to move out. He got up and fond that the camp guard had made him some coffee. As he sat there by the fire drinking his coffee others took down his tent. This was one benefit of being in command. You did not set up or take down your own tent. Others did it for you.

The day before Scott had sent out spies in all directions to help him find Lopez. Two went north into Thorton and then Groesbeck. Three others went on to Marquez. When the Texicans were about half way between Kosse and Marquez the spies he sent to Marquez returned with news. For some reason Lopez was heading north to Jewett.

There were no shortcuts for the Texicans to use to help them catch up with Lopez. They had no choice but to just fallow but in order to catch Lopez they would have to continue moving and stop setting up and taking down camps. The Texicans pushed on to Marquez without stopping. They traveled for two days and one night but finally got closer to Lopez. The problem with this was that the Texicans were nattered to fight if they had to.

Seeing the mistake he made in pushing his militia to hard Scott stopped he Texicans just north of Marquez on Highway 79. There they rested while Scott sent out more spies to Jewett. The next day the Texican Militia would move closer to Jewett but these spies were to find out what was going in Jewett and report back to Scott.

The next morning Scott had the Texican Militia break camp before daylight. Even though he was busy Paula brought Scott his MRE breakfast. He was hungry so he ate it as he walked around giving orders. By time the eastern sky was turning babble color they were off towards Jewett again.

The next night the Texicans had made it to the school grounds half way between Marquez and Jewett. That was where one of the three spies Scott sent to Jewett reported back to him.

The other two spies had been shot. The woman was shot for not allowing a Mexican soldier rape her and the man was shot for defending her. The one that was reporting to Scott only survived by hiding in the bushes and not trying to defend the woman with them. He told Scott that he felt like a coward but he had to report back. He could not do that if he was also dead. Scott told him that he did the right thing.

Although the spy never saw Lopez over one hundred of his soldiers were still in Jewett. After what he saw happen to his two friends he was afraid of going into the town itself and watched for a while from trees outside of town. Scott had the Texicans break camp and get ready to move out. Hours before it even got daylight the Texicans were on the move.

By noon Scott, Paula, and Nelson were hidden in the bushes just outside of the town of Jewett. Because the road curved in town they could not see very deep into town. In that short distance Scott watched as men were shot right in the middle of he street. An old woman was beat to death for God knows what reason. One young girl was raped right in front of other Mexican soldiers that stood there and laughed.

Everything in Scott wanted to call the Texicans in to just charge the town and stop all of the things going on but he knew he had to have a plan of attack. They went back to the others about half a mile away and Scott called his Captains together.

Before getting to close to Jewett Scott sent Companies A and B north on Highway 39. They would go only a few blocks before turning north to walk through the western part of town. Companies C and D had it harder as they had to walk through the thick trees and brush to line for their walk through the eastern part of town. Company E and Bailey's Snipers, as they called themselves, walked right down main street which was also Highway 79. Scott brought up the rear as another sniper.

By this time Captain Waters' Company E of young people had sixty one soldiers under the age of nineteen and they were all looking to finally do some fighting. However; most of them had not yet been tested in battle and Scott was not sure how they would react.

Scott got on his radio to all of the Captains and ordered them all to move in. Their orders were simple. Kill all Mexicans wearing brown uniforms and carrying rifles.

As the Texican Militia started moving into Jewett the people that lived there stayed hidden in their homes. Finally a gunshot was heard and all hell broke loose. Within seconds of he first gunshot the entire town was under attack.

Companies A and B were moving through town faster than the rest of the Texicans because the west side of town was mostly homes of those that lived there. There was very little resistance. Companies C and D met up with little resistance as the Mexican soldiers had their camp set up there. Company E and Bailey's Snipers found less resistance than Scott expected.

After quickly moving through the western part of town Companies A and B turned right to come into downtown itself. After contacting Scott to let him know that they were coming in he moved in closer to the action. Waters spread out his company to cover both sides of main street. The fighting was furious but something was wrong.

Later Companies C and Do turned left and came into town squeezing what Mexican soldiers that were left out the northern part of town. Within two hours after moving into the town of Jewett the battle was over. The Texicans had captured only seven of the Mexican soldiers.

The Texicans set up camp for the rest of the night. As Scott sat in his chair Nelson gave him her report. Seven of the Mexican soldiers had been captured and three of them were badly wounded. The Texicans lost fourteen with another ten wounded. When Nelson added the dead Mexican soldiers with the wounded and captured ones she realized that they only had one hundred twenty. Another one hundred were missing including Lopez.

The prisoners were brought to Scott. He wore his usual red die to try to scare them into thinking that he really was the devil; El Diablo. When the prisoners saw him they fell to their knees begging him to let them go. They did not want El Diablo to take their souls to Hell.

Two of the wounded prisoners died of their wounds. The other one was there with the other four. After questioning them Scott had the four that had not been wounded executed. The wounded prisoner begged El Diablo to show mercy on him. Finally Scott agreed to do as the soldier asked.

With another Texican interpreting Scott spoke to the prisoner. "I will show you this mercy you asked for but you will do something for me." The prisoner agreed. "You will find Lopez. Tell him what you saw here and then tell him that I am coming for him and anyone that is with him."

The prisoner was given food and water and then released right there in the middle of town. Scott had him watched to see which direction he went. That way the Texicans would know which direction Lopez was. As Scott suspected, the Mexican soldier ran north on Highway 79; towards Buffalo.

The Texicans spent that night in Jewett. As Scott sat by his campfire he talked with his Captains. They all wanted to end this thing with Lopez as quickly as they could. Suddenly there were a few gunshots heard not far away. Those checking the area came up with no one but, Scott and Captain Causk of Company C were hit. Causk was only shot in the arm but Scott took a bullet to his left shoulder. He was out cold.

Nelson ordered the area searched again for the snipers that shot Scott and Causk. This time one man was brought in but three others with sniper rifles were killed. The man was a white American that was part of a group that did not want Texas to become republic.

With Scott down Captain Peg Nelson assumed command. When the captured man refused to answer any of her questions she had him shot. Then she had guards set out all around the town.

The bullet was removed from Scott's shoulder. He would be okay but he would not be able to hold up a rifle for a while if ever again. The entire time that he was being operated on Paula held his hand.

Not to many of the Texicans got any sleep that night. Those that were not on guard around town could not sleep because they were worried about Scott. The operation went well and Paula remained at his side holding his hand.

By time the sun came up the next morning Scott was already awake. He had help but he managed to get to his chair by the campfire. Paula made him a pot of coffee and in minutes he sat there sipping on his coffee. Then Nelson came to him.

"You ready to take back over Sir?" Nelson asked.

"Yes but ..." Scott said. "... I need to talk with you."

"Yes Sir." Nelson said as she sat down close to Scott.

Scott and Captain Nelson devised a plan for the Texicans to attack Lopez in Buffalo. They had to do it quickly before he left again. Lopez had a habit of inviting Scott into a fight and then not being there when Scott got there. This time he wanted to catch Lopez.

The only thing different with this attack was that Scott would be staying behind while Nelson took the Texicans into battle. Captain Waters and his Company E would also stay behind for Scott's protection. Some of his company were killed in the attack on Jewett but he still had fifty two left.

Lopez only had just over one hundred soldiers while the

Texicans still had just under five hundred without Company E. Captain Nelson talked with the other Captains and they go ready to move out. The trucks were unloaded so that the Texicans could be taken to within a mile of Buffalo. Once Companies A and b were there they would attack. Companies C and D would be carried there as quickly as possible.

By midnight all of Companies A and B were dropped off. As they walked closer to the town of Buffalo more and more of companies C and D arrived. By 0200 hours all four companies were within a quarter of a mile from the outskirts of Buffalo.

Scott sat back at camp listening to the radio and was amazed at how well Nelson was doing. Of course Paula was there bringing him cups of coffee and an MRE for breakfast. Having put most of his company on the Buffalo side of town to protect Scott from any of the Mexicans that came back a few were on the opposite side of town.

Then suddenly the words came over the radio; "Taking fire." Nelson was giving orders and the captains were ordering their companies into different positions. Finally the fight to catch or kill Lopez was on.

The Texicans quickly moved up to Interstate 45. They found very little resistance until then but fighting past the interstate was another story. In one battle Captain Causk said that he had lost three fighters. In another battle Captain Sales of Company A mentioned loosing seven fighters. The Texicans were loosing men but so was Lopez.

Eventually, Companies A and D moved around behind Lopez and his soldiers and kept them from escaping again. They were surrounded. As the Texicans continued to fire on the trapped Mexican soldiers Scott set back at camp with anticipation. It looked like Scott would finally get to meet Lopez.

Finally the shooting stopped and the remaining nine Mexican soldiers were captured. Captain Nelson reported by radio to Scott that the prisoners were all smiling. Scott ordered her to transport the prisoners back to him with plenty of security. Using two of the trucks she had the prisoners transported back to Scott with part of Company C as guard. In the meantime the dead were searched to find Lopez.

Lopez was not found among the dead so he had to be among the prisoners. When the two trucks got back to the camp in Jewett Scott watched as they unloaded. He was shocked when the last prisoner was unloaded and there was still no Lopez. When the dead and prisoners were counted Scott found out that Lopez and about ten of his soldiers had somehow escaped again. There was one more thing that some of the prisoners mentioned that bothered Scott.

As Scott questioned the prisoners he learned that Lopez and about ten of his soldiers had escaped. That was why the captives were smiling. They had kept the Texicans fighting while Lopez escaped again. Knowing that if captured they would most assuredly be executed for helping Lopez getaway from El Diablo again. However; two of them were terrified about meeting El Diablo and they talked.

Scott rubbed on more of the red die before questioning the Mexican prisoners in order to scare the Mexican soldiers. Then he walked out to them without his bandages and sling. He could not allow them to see him wounded. After all. Who could hurt the Devil?

"I am getting tired of being thought of as the Devil." Scott said to Paula. "I'm a Christian not a Satanist."

"But it's the fear of going to Hell that scares them." Paula said.

"I know but still ..." Scott remarked. I was thinking about The Angel of Death."

As Scott sat in his chair he looked over the prisoners that were brought before him. With a wave of his hand the prisoners were forced to their knees. He was very disappointed to see that Lopez in fact was not among the prisoners. But where did he go? How did he even get away?

As Scott questioned the prisoners he only found two that would talk. He also saw that they were terrified of him. Actually they were terrified of being sent to Hell. He had to get answers and he wanted those answers quickly before Lopez got to far away.

One by one Scott had the prisoners shot for not talking making sure that he saved the two scared ones for last. By time all of the prisoners were shot except for them they was talking, telling Scott anything he wanted to know.

Come to find out Lopez took ten of his soldiers south on Interstate 45 before the Texicans could close in and surround the other Mexican soldiers. Then he heard a name that got his attention. One of the two prisoners mentioned a man that came in and started helping Lopez. The man called himself Major Layton.

Now Layton had betrayed the Republic of Texas and was not helping the enemy. That was all Scott needed to kill the man on sight. After he finished questioning the two prisoners Scott had them fed and given water. Then he released them and again watched which direction they went. They instantly headed south out of Jewett.

Scott knew that by that time Lopez and Layton had already passed them again. Even if they broke camp right then they would not be able to get to the interstate in Centerville before Lopez and Layton passed by. He allowed the Texicans to rest the next day. They would leave the day after that.

Then that night Scott got a report from a small group of people that just came from Groesbeck. When they turned off of Highway 164 onto Highway 39 they passed a small group of Mexican soldiers. A white man was with them and he was not a prisoner. The Mexicans were coming from the east but they did not pay attention to which direction they went.

This meant that Lopez could have gone to Groesbeck or turned north on Highway 39 and gone on to Mexia. Scott wondered why Lopez was not heading home to Mexico for more troops and to re-supply. He knew that Lopez was up to something but what could it be?

The two prisoners must have lied to Scott to throw him off. They must have wanted Scott to go in the opposite direction so

Lopez could get away. Then again; what if the prisoners did not lie and the small group coming out of Groesbeck were mistaken? No! The small group of people described Lopez and Layton to well. That was the direction they went.

Scott called for Captain Nelson. When she got to his campfire he told her that they Texicans would be taking Highway 39 the next morning up towards Highway 164. After that he had no idea which direction to go. Nelson left the camp and told the other Captains what to expect the next morning. Then she returned to Scott and reported that all of the company leaders knew.

Chapter 14

Lopez

Scott was tired of Lopez getting away all of the time. Now Layton was with Lopez making it even more important to catch up with them. Why would Layton join forces with Lopez after Lopez wiped out Layton's militia anyway? Something was wrong and Scott could not figure it out.

The Texicans broke camp before daylight. By time the sun was coming up they were already on Highway 39 heading north. Scott sent three spies into Groesbeck and three more into Mexia to try to find out which direction Lopez went.

As the Texicans moved northward Scott got word that the Texicans were running out of food. He talked with Captain Waters and asked how many of his young fighters could hunt. Only twenty of the fifty two fighters had any experience hunting. Scott asked that those twenty start hunting to bring food to the Texicans. Scott also gave one of the trucks to Waters for hauling the food back to the Texican camp.

Four days after leaving Jewett the Texicans reached Highway 164 and set up camp there. Scott told the six spies to meet them there. While there the Texicans would cut and dry the meat brought in and get some more rest. Half of the Texicans were over the age of fifty so they got tired quicker that the young did.

The first night that the Texicans were at the crossroads of Highways 164 and 39 Scott sat in his usual folding chair and watched the fire burning. Captain Sales was roasting a deer ham over the fire which would feed all of the officers. More venison and wild hogs meat was being cooked over other campfires. The little bit of meat that could be shot had to feed five hundred forty two fighters. Things were getting so bad that Scott decided to go back to Central Command for more MREs.

After leaving Captain Nelson in charge Scott, Paula, and six of the fighters from Company E left the Texican camp for Dallas. They took one of the trucks with them to haul back the MREs.

That night a bad storm hit the Texicans. Discouraged over not having enough food and thinking that Scott had abandoned them all many of the Texicans deserted. By time Scott got to Dallas almost one hundred of the Texicans were gone. Of course Scott did not know all of this was going on. This bothered Captain Nelson as she saw it as her not doing a good job. She got so depressed that she also almost deserted rather than facing Scott when he got back.

When Scott's group drove into the Central Command Compound they saw many other trucks leaving. He had the Humvee and truck pull up close to supply and got out. Then he had the six men stand by while he and Paula saw the Colonel.

Ax soon as Scott and Paula walked into the Colonel's office Melon came down on him. "I don't want to hear it again Major."

Scott stopped on the spot. He had no idea what the Colonel was talking about. "What do you mean Sir?" he asked.

"Word has it that you killed Layton."

"No Sir. " Scott insisted. "He's still alive."

Colonel Melon stopped what he was doing and looked at Scott. "You sure about that?"

"Yes Sir." Scott admitted. "Lopez wiped out his militia and I have been chasing him. Now Layton has joined forces with Lopez. We attacked Lopez's remaining forces in Jewett and Buffalo. He now only has about ten men with him along with Layton which is helping him."

"Are you sure that Layton is helping him?" Melon asked.

"I honestly can't say Sir but he is with Lopez." Scott said.

Colonel Melon thought for a moment and then asked; "Why are you here?"

"I have about five hundred fifty fighters and food shard to find." Scott told Melon. "We are sticking in one place so we can hunt for our food and there is very little wild game to hunt."

"Did you see those trucks leaving out a few minutes ago?" Melon asked Scott.

"Yes Sir."

"Those trucks were taking the last of the MREs." Melon advised. "We have no food here."

Scott was shocked. What could he do now? Pleading with the different towns they went through was the only thing left. But many of them were barely surviving also so they would not be able to help.

"I'm sorry." Melon said. "Unless you need anything else I'm really busy."

"No Sir." Scott said. "I'll feed my fighters one way or another."

"That's what the other Militia leaders are doing." Melon advised.

Scott turned to Paula as they walked towards the office door. Then he whipped around and asked; "Could we get some M-16s and ammunition?"

"Yeah sure." Melon said. Then he got on the radio and ordered supply to give Scott a few rifles and ammunition. "Now get out'a here."

By time Scott and Paula got down to the truck it had already been loaded. He looked in the back of the truck and saw two crates of M-16s and three crates of ammunition. Then he thought he would try something.

"What the hell is this?" He asked the young man in supply.

"The Colonel said to give you a few M-16s so I did." the man said.

"He didn't say a few he said two ... as in two thousand." Scott tried to conthe young man.

"I can let you have two hundred but no way can I give you two thousand rifles."

Scott pretended to be disgusted. "Can you at least let me have four hundred?"

The man thought for a moment and then agreed. Scott looked over at Paula who was trying to figure out what Scott was doing.

"And I need ammunition for all of those rifles too."

The man yelled from behind a stack of crates; "Yes Sir." Then he stuck his head out from behind the crates and added; "I'll take care of you Sir."

Scott walked over to Paula whose mouth hung open. She could not figure out what Scott was doing and how he was getting all of the rifles and ammunition. He just looked at her and smiled.

Thirty minutes later the truck was loaded. Scott got got four hundred M-16 rifles and forty crates of ammunition. He signed the paperwork and jumped into his Humvee. Then they left as quickly as possible. Because of the storm that was still coming down it took them just over four hours to get back to the Texicans.

When the truck pulled up many of the Texicans pulled the back flaps open hoping to find food. Imagine their disappointment when they saw the truck full of crates of M-16s and ammunition. The rain stopped and Scott stood on a stump and yelled out to the Texicans telling them an idea he had.

Scott told everyone that Central Command had not food of any kind but they had plenty of M-16 rifles and ammunition. He wanted to start by going to Groesbeck and arming the people there. He would teach them how to defend themselves and their town. In return he wanted them to feed his fighters. Within a few hours of his speech most of the Texicans had agreed. They still lost another forty Texicans that sneaked off during the night. Only three hundred eighty nine Texicans remained.

Scott, Paula, and the six from Company E that went to Dallas with them went ahead to Groesbeck. Captain Nelson brought the Texicans into Groesbeck two days later. When Scott and the others got to Groesbeck he had everyone come to city hall to talk with them. There on the front lawn he tried to make a deal with them. He would arm them all with M-16s and plenty of ammunition if they would feed his Texicans. As more towns joined in the deal the burden of feeding them would lessen. They all agreed.

The next day Scott and Paula taught the few people left in Groesbeck how to use the M-16 rifle and how to fight. By time Captain Nelson got to Groesbeck with the Texicans the people of Groesbeck were a well oiled fighting machine. The people started bringing in all kinds of food that they could spare. Dried rice and beans, flour and other things were among the food brought. Two large cast iron pots were also donated to the Texicans.

Word got out to other towns about what the Texicans had done with Groesbeck and some of them wanted in on the deal. Before long the towns of Jewett and Mart agreed to supply food for the remaining guns and ammunition. After Groesbeck there were enough guns and ammunition to supply Jewett and mart but that was all. These three towns giving them food made it much easier to get food as they were spread out from each other.

By mid July the Texicans were set for food but they still had no idea where Lopez and Layton had gone. Then one day a man and woman came through Groesbeck and told Scott that they met up with a Mexicans whose last name was Lopez. He was making fun of El Diablo who he had escaped from more than once. Then the man said that this Lopez was in Flynn.

Scott talked it over with his Captains as to whether or not the Texicans should go after Lopez again. They all agreed that it had to be done. The next morning the Texicans broke camp and headed towards Flynn. What Scott did not know was that the man and woman were spies sent out by Lopez. Lopez was setting a trap to ambush El Diablo. And finish him off for good.

As the Texicans started to leave Groesbeck something kept telling Scott to hold back. However; like the others he wanted both Lopez and Layton bad. He always fallowed his gut feelings but this time he didn't. Something was wrong but he could not tell what it was. His drive to catch Lopez and Layton overwhelmed his reasoning.

It took three days for the Texicans to reach Jewett. Scott had sent out three spies to check ahead and report to him in Jewett. However; when they got to Jewett the spies were not there. As

Scott sat by his campfire that night in Jewett he still had that something nagging at him. Something was wrong but he could not put his finger on it.

That night Scott talked with Captain Sales of Company A. He told Sales that he had a bad feeling about something ahead but could not figure out what it was. Sales volunteered to take his company on ahead to try to find the three spies. If they ran into trouble then he would send word back to Scott. Scott agreed and Captain Sales left with his Texican fighters for Marquez.

For the rest of the night Scott could not sleep. He was up and down all night; sitting at the campfire and back to bed. Finally at one of the times when he was up Paula came out of her tent to sit with him.

"What's wrong?" Paula asked Scott.

"I just have a bad feeling about moving ahead and going after Lopez and Layton." Scott told her. "Something is ... I have ... I don't know what it is."

"You okay Sir?" the camp guard asked as he walked by.

"Just can't sleep." Scott replied.

"It's almost daylight Sir. You want me to make some coffee for you?" the guard asked.

"Yeah ... I guess so." Scott agreed with a smile.

"I'll get it." Paula said as she got up and got the coffee pot.

"Yes Ma'am." the guard replied and then continued walking around camp.

About twenty minutes later Scott and Paula were sipping on their coffee. The Texicans were busy breaking camp to move out to Marquez. As everyone started moving out of the area the medic checked Scott's shoulder. He had been feeling bad for a while with more pain to his wounded shoulder that usual.

As the medic feared, Scott's shoulder was infected. The medic cleaned the wound but he also instructed Scott that his body needed to rest. He had to stop for a while and allow his body to heal his shoulder. But Scott only had one thing on his mind; getting Lopez and Layton.

By that evening the Texicans made it to the school and

camped for the night. As Scott sat by his fire Company A was having problems in Marquez. They had walked into a trap.

Company A walked into Marquez not knowing that Lopez had set up a trap to try and kill Scott. As Company A was caught out in the open they found nothing to hide behind. By time they made it to any cover half of them had already been shot. No matter what Captain Sales did his fighters were killed. Finally Sales and two other men were captured.

The three Texicans were shown the bodies of the three spies that Scott had sent there. Then he pulled his sword and cutoff he head of one of the men captured with Sales. After yelling at Sales Lopez cut his head off as well. Lopez was about to cut the head off of the last prisoner when Layton whispered in his ear.

One of the men with Lopez grabbed Sale's head and dropped it in a pillow case. Then it was given to the last prisoner who was told to take it to Scott with this warning. "Go away or this will happen to you."

The medic wanted Scott to stop and rest a few days but there was no way that was going to happen with Lopez being so close. When the next morning came the Texicans were moving before it was even daylight. They had only gone about two miles when the last of the spies caught up with them.

Barely able to stand the spy was given some water. He handed the pillow case to Scott but begged him not to look inside. Scott opened the pillow case and looked inside anyway. Seeing the head of Captain Sales in the pillow case bothered him a great deal. The spy then told Scott that the three spies were also dead. Then he said something that shocked Scott. Lopez now had about forty to fifty Mexicans with him.

The spy said that he overheard someone say something about MS-13 helping him so that had to be where the extra soldiers came from. Even if Lopez did have about fifty five soldiers the Texicans still numbered at just over three hundred. Scott ordered Company B to walk about one quarter of a mile ahead of the others. Then the other Texicans fallowed.

As Company B walked into Marquez they kept their eyes

open for any ambushes. They did not see the two Browning fifty caliber machine guns set up on both sides of he highway. As Company B walked past the two machine guns the Mexicans opened fire. Within seconds Company B was no more.

As Company C and D ran into the town they were cut down. Scott did not send them in but they just did it. Captain Waters and his Company E stayed back with Scott. As the survivors of Companies C and D ran back the guns stopped.

Within a few minutes the Texicans had been reduced to about eighty and over fifty of them were below the age of nineteen. Scott had the Texicans retreat about a mile and then regroup. Keeping twenty of Company E's fighters to protect him Scott split the others to become part of Companies C and D. Then he sent Company C into the woods on the eastern side of he highway and Company D on the western side. They would work their way behind the fifty caliber machine guns to capture them.

Then Scott rubbed on some of the red die hoping to scare at least one of the Mexicans with Lopez. Then he and the others with him moved down the highway to draw attention to them allowing the two companies to get behind the Browning machine guns.

Scott took a few steps and then stopped. He had the others spread out even into the ditches on both sides of the highway. He continued to move ahead a few steps at a time, stopping for a while and then continuing for a few more steps. This gave Companies C and D time to get to the Machine guns. Suddenly there was some gunfire on the left as Company C found their target. Then the Browning on the right started firing short bursts at the Texicans across the highway. Then gunfire opened up from the Texicans on the right. Both Browning Machine guns were taken. Scott moved his group up quickly.

When the dead and prisoners were gathered both Lopez and Layton were missing. Suddenly there was three gunshots from behind Scott. He whipped around to see Paula and two of her snipers firing at four to five men running down Highway 7 towards Robbins. They only shot one which was quickly captured.

The wounded man was brought to Scott. With Scott still wearing the red die the man thought that he was looking at the devil himself. He spoke English well and admitted that he was part of a MS-13 gang out of College Station but they had joined; and he said proudly; "Brigade General Lopez." So one of the men running had to have been Lopez. One of the others was surely Layton.

The Texicans only had two hundred five fighters left but plenty of supplies. Scott sent Captain Divings and his Company D after Lopez and Layton as the rest of the Texicans rested. Divings only had nine fighters left in it but a smaller group can move faster than a larger group can.

Captain Causk argued with Scott about sending out so few. Lopez was very resourceful and would probably overtake them as he had Companies A and B. Scott finally got so tired of her nagging that he yelled and ordered her to shut up. Then Paula grabbed Scott around the waste and stopped him.

Looking into Scott's eyes Paul said; "You know she's right."

Scott let out a heavy sigh. "I know but I don't want to be left with just a few fighters here with me." Then he turned to Captain Causk and told her to do as she wanted. Then he called Captain Divings and told him that Company D would be coming up behind them.

The infection in Scott's shoulder was getting so that it was tapping all of his energy. He had the others set up camp in Marquez where they would wait for word from Companies C and D. Scott was in bad shape and he knew it. The medic told him that he had to allow his body and especially his shoulder to rest and now he had no choice. Once his tent was set up he went straight to bed. Paula sat in a chair beside his bed until he fell asleep.

The remaining Texicans understood Scott's need to stop and heal. He was not the first one to get sicker and weak from infection. Infection was usually considered a way of life out in the field. It is dirty and cold; perfect conditions for bacteria to grow.

Scott slept until noon the next day. When he did get up it was against Paula's wishes.

"But you need to stay in bed." Paula insisted as she tried to hold him down.

"If you looked on my lapel ... okay there's nothing there but ... I am still a Major." Scott said. "You're not even a Captain anymore."

"But you need your rest ... Sir."

Oh!" Scott replied. "Now it's Sir."

"But you ..." Paula said before being outranked again.

"Remove your hand from me ... woman." Scott yelled loud enough that everyone heard.

Paula backed up and Scott sat up on the side of his bed. She stood there as Scott tried three times to stand. Then she called in two men to help him get up and get dressed. Then they helped him walk outside to his chair. One of the men built up the campfire and a pot of cold coffee was moved so it could warm up.

Just minutes later Companies C and D walked into camp with three prisoners. It was Lopez and two of the other MS-13 gang members that joined him. Scott wanted so bad to stand but he couldn't do it.

Lopez and the other two were brought in front of Scott and forced to their knees. Lopez laughed at Scott's illness. Some of the red die was still on Scott's face so the two Mexicans were not sure what to think.

"You looking ... sick." Lopez barely said. Then he laughed again.

"You speak English now." Scott mentioned.

"I learned a ... much your language from ... your friend."

"Which friend is that?" Scott asked.

"Major Layton." Lopez said with a smile.

Scott looked deep into Lopez's eyes and asked; "Where is he?"

"No know but not tell you if I did." Lopez said.

Scott was feeling sicker. He knew that he should have stayed in bed. Before passing out he gave one last order. "Execute all

three of them."

Two of the Texicans had to almost carry Scott back to his bed where Paula stripped him and put him to bed. He was very sick and finally he knew it. He did not even wakeup with three gunshots were fired just fifty feet away. He slept well knowing that he finally got Lopez. Now to find Layton.

Chapter 15

Layton

Scott slept until the next morning but, this time he stayed in bed. The Texicans were held up there in Marquez for three more days as Scott healed and gained his strength. On the forth morning after executing Lopez Scott got up from his bed on his own. Paula sat in her chair watching him as he stood and got dressed. This time she said nothing.

Scott stopped just long enough to look into her eyes and say; "It's time to find Layton."

It was still dark when Scott stepped outside of his tent. "Captain Nelson." he yelled out as loud as he could. A minutes later a half dressed Captain Nelson stood in front of Scott. "Break camp now." he continued to yell to everyone that could hear him. "We leave out in one hour." Nelson stood there wondering if there was anything else. "Now Captain ... right now." he yelled again.

"Father." Scott said right there in the middle of camp. *"I need to find Layton but he has a five day head start. He could be anyplace by now. Please help me to find him."*

By daybreak the Texicans were ready to leave Marquez. He was going to head down towards Robins where Layton was seen running a few days earlier. But something kept telling him to go back to Jewett so he did.

The Texicans numbered at two hundred five; not a big army in any since. They were now just going after one man but he could have found help by now. When they reached Jewett Scott found out that Layton had been through there the day before. The woman that told Scott about this strange man she met also said that he was on his way to Mexia. Therefore; the Texicans were on their way to Mexia as well.

As the Texicans moved towards Mexia Scott learned that Layton was recruiting for his militia. However; his militia was mostly young people that were against the republic of Texas.

"Here we go again." Scott said to Paula after telling her about the last time this happened. "Young people from all around were joining this movement to fight against the Republic of Texas. Then when it came down to fighting they just sat on the ground and cried."

Scott hoped that these young people would do the same. He got into this war to fight UN troops coming into Texas. Then the Liberal/Communist president turned dictator gave Texas to Mexico so he started fighting Mexican soldiers trying to take the state. Then Governor Davis of the new Texas called for fighters to defend the Republic of Texas but, Scott never signed up to kill young people. He did not realize how a confusing war this one had been until then.

A few days later the Texicans reached Highway 164 and stopped to camp for the night. As the Texicans worked to set up camp a small group of young people came through on their way to Mexia. They were on their way to meet with others like them and a man that would lead them into peace.

"So this is now a peace movement." Scott mentioned as he smiled.

"Well ... I guess it is." one of the women in the group agreed.

"I know this man you are going to see." Scott said. "He is not a good man."

"We have heard that he is a great man." the woman said. "He speaks of peace after fighting those that want Texas to be a republic."

"What's wrong with Texas becoming a republic?" Scott asked.

"Texas belongs to Mexico now." he woman insisted. "We need to except that."

"Why?" Scott asked. "Why should we just give in and do

that? Why should we not fight for our freedom?"

Suddenly the woman grabbed one of the Texican's rifles and jerked it from his hands. Then the others tried to take other weapons. "You're the enemy." the woman yelled as she raised the rifle she had towards Scott's face.

A gunshot rang out from behind Scott and the woman fell to the ground. Paula saw what was coming and stood there with her rifle ready. Once the other young people saw their friend dead they stopped fighting. Scott was right. They still had no stomach for fighting and especially dying.

"The rest of you go home." Scott ordered them. "We are on our way to kill this man ... Layton. I know this man. He is not any kind of a good man."

The young people left the Texican camp but no one paid any attention to which direction they went. Instead of going back to Buffalo where they came they continued on their way to Mexia. In two days they would be in Mexia and Layton would know that the Texicans were on their way to get him.

Scott had no idea that the young people continued on to Mexia nor that Layton knew they were coming. This gave Layton time to set up a few ambushes. Layton was tired of the Texicans budding in on everything he wanted to do. He was going to end it one way or another. The funny thing about that was that Scott was thinking the same thing.

That night Scott sat by his campfire watching the flames jump around. Paula sat in a chair beside him and held onto his arm. For a while neither said a thing. Then Paula asked what he was thinking.

"I was just looking at the flames jumping around." Scott said. "Have you ever noticed how the flames keep jumping around. The only thing that changes the flames is when a log shifts or burns down. With that log in a different position the flames then change ... and only then."

"Are you okay Scott?" Paula asked.

Scott smiled and said; "I'm fine."

The next morning the Texicans moved out again on their way

to Mexia. It was not even daylight but Scott wanted to get into Mexia before it got to hot. The Texicans were getting tired of these very early wakeups and leaving for another place to search for someone else. They joined the Texicans to fight for a free Republic of Texas not to chase someone allover the place. The way they saw it if Scott wanted Layton so bad then he could go after the man. Before the Texicans left that morning Scott realized that just over fifty of the Texicans left during the night. Only one hundred fifty Texicans were left. Thirty more left during the next two hours after leaving for Mexia. By time the Texicans got within two miles of Mexia only eighty Texicans remained.

All of Captain Waters' Company E was still with Scott. All of Paula's snipers and about twenty of Company C were also there. Scott had never been so depressed. But even with eighty Texicans they should be able to take one man unless Layton had new friends.

Scott had all of the Texicans spread out as they walked into Mexia. There was no sign of Layton but there were many young people around. Scott warned the others to keep an eye on all the young people because they did not know who to trust. That evening they reached the old National Guard Armory. That was when all hell broke loose.

Gunfire opened up on the Texicans from the left, right, and in front. The Texicans returned fire as they looked for any cover but, there was no cover to be found. As the Texicans scattered their numbers quickly dropped. Scott busted a store's glass door and ran in with a few of the Texicans close behind him.

After a few minutes the gunfire outside finally stopped. Scott looked around a display case and saw Layton standing outside.

"Come on out Scotty boy." Layton yelled. "I know you're in there." Layton waited a while and then yelled again. "If you don't come out I'm gon'a kill the prisoners including your girlfriend."

Scott told the Texicans with him to remain there until it got dark. Then he wanted them to get out of town. "I'm coming out."

Scott yelled at Layton.

"Get rid of your rifle before you step out here." Layton said.

Scott dropped his rifle and stepped outside. The sun was so bright that he was blinded for a moment or two. Then his eyes adjusted and he saw all of the dead Texicans. Then he saw the captured Texicans but Paula was not among them. *Was she one of the dead?* he thought to himself.

"Come on out Scott." Layton ordered him.

Scott slowly stepped out to the road and stopped. He looked around and saw that Layton had already recruited more of the young people than Scott thought. Layton only had about fifteen armed young people with him and yet they killed over fifty of the Texicans. *But where were the others?*

Layton looked at the young people standing behind the captured Texicans and ordered them to kill the prisoners.

"No." Scott yelled as the captured Texicans were shot in the back. "You said you would not shoot them."

"No I didn't." Layton insisted. "I just told you to come out or I would shoot them. After you came out I didn't need them anymore so I had them shot anyway."

"You're an evil son of a whore." Scott yelled as two of Layton's people held him down on his knees.

As Layton walked around a little he asked; "Now what to do with you." Layton walked a little more and then said; "I have it. We'll kill you."

"Others are also looking for you and someday they will find you." Scott said.

"Maybe so but not today." Layton replied. Then he stepped over to Scott and pulled his pistol. "Good-by Scott."

Not being tied Scott lunged out at Layton and grabbed the pistol. The two men wrestled for a few second before Layton's people pulled Scott off of him. As Scott lay there Layton pointed his pistol at Scott's head.

Suddenly a shot rang out from down the road and Layton fell to the ground with a bullet hole in his head. Then other gunshots came from down the road and a few of the young people started falling. Scott grabbed a pistol laying on the ground in front of him and started firing. Within thirty seconds of the first shot the shooting stopped as the remaining young people ran for their lives.

Paula and her snipers along with a few of the others ran up to Scott. As the medic looked at Scott's shoulder two of the Texicans went back and got the trucks. When the trucks got to Scott they loaded him into one of he trucks and left the area. There were only sixteen Texicans now and they all were able to ride in the trucks. When the Texicans reached the crossroads of Highways 39 and 164 they pulled over and set up camp.

With all of the objectives out of the way Scott had to think of what to do next. Recruiting was a for sure thing and that was best done in Dallas. People wanting to join a militia went to Central Command in Dallas. It was easier than trying to find a militia.

Scott called for Captain Nelson not realizing that she had been killed. With the two remaining companies that looked more like squads Scott gave Paula the rank of Captain again and placed her over all companies. Dale powers was promoted to Captain and was put in charge of the snipers.

That night as Scott and Paula sit by the campfire he looked over at her and said; "I'm getting to old for this. I need to find an easier job."

"Well Colonel Melon did offer you two jobs." she reminded him. "Layton took the one putting him in charge of all militias but ... I really don't think he has that job anymore."

Scott thought for a while and then made a decision on what to do next. They would go to Central Command in Dallas. He would give his report to Colonel Melon and try to recruit more fighters and get more supplies. They would leave out for Dallas the next morning.

The last of the gasoline was put in the trucks. If there was no gasoline to pass out then at least get the trucks back to Central Command. Even if there was no supplies they would find out what was going on and they could get some new Texicans.

The next morning Scott got up just before daylight. He

allowed everyone to sleep in a few hours. As he sat in his chair by the campfire Paula joined him. She asked him if he might take a job at Central Command if one was offered him. He only said that he might. Around 0900 hours he got everyone up. A hour later they were off to Central Command.

Not running into any problems the Texicans pulled into Central Command just four hours after leaving their last camp. The two trucks were marked with the word "Texican" so it would not be taken by anyone else or moved into the supply parking lot. Then Scott and Paula went up to see the Colonel while the others stayed with the trucks.

As soon as Scott stepped in Melon's office the Colonel yelled out for someone to grab Scott. Three soldiers there grabbed Scott and held him.

"What the hell?" Scott yelled.

"You're under arrest for the murder of Major Layton.

"Murder?" Scott yelled out. "You fucking idiot. He's been trying to kill me. Then he joined forces with Brigade General Lopez. He helped Lopez to almost wipe out my militia. I have a few left standing by my trucks outside. Then just before he pulled the trigger to kill me he was shot."

Colonel Melon looked around the room and then at Scott. "Release him." he ordered.

"What's going on Sir?" Scott asked.

"Layton came through here about a week or so ago saying that you were trying to kill him." Melon said. "Then I got word that you murdered him a few days ago."

"He was shot as he held a pistol to my head." Scott told everyone there. "He was a split second from pulling the trigger when he got shot."

"I am the one that shot him Sir." Paula said. "Like the Major said … Layton was about to kill him when I pulled my trigger before he did."

"Well it doesn't matter anyway." Melon said. "The war is over."

"Which one?" Scott asked.

"The war with Mexico." Melon advised. "England, France, and Israel all threatened to start helping us fight for our freedom if Mexico did not stop invading us. The details are being worked outright now and there is no formal peace treaty signed yet but ... Mexico agreed to stop sending troops across the river and into the new Republic of Texas."

Scott and Paula hugged each other and she even shocked him with a quick kiss. "What about UN troops trying to cross our northern borders? Scott asked.

"The dictator running the United States now is backing them off some." Melon said. "There is word that he wants Texas back now but no one knows for sure."

"Our President Davis has called for a new election." one of the other men in the room mentioned.

"What's this?" Scott asked.

"President Davis is getting old and has said that he will allow an election in a few months for president of the new Republic of Texas." Melon commented. "If you want to start taking it easier now I still have those two jobs open."

Scott smiled and said; "I don't think so."

"What are you going to do now?" Melon asked.

As Scott and Paula were walking out of he room he stopped and turned to face his Colonel. "I'm running for President of the new Republic of Texas."

Mexico ended up signing a peace treaty with the New Republic of Texas and never sent their troops across the border into the new republic again. They even went as far as signing into the treaty that they would not allow any other country to cross their land for the purpose of invading the new Republic of Texas.

The Dictator president of the United States moved a few of the UN troops back away from the northern border of the new republic only for a show. Within weeks they were back. Because of this England, France, and Israel left the United Nations and chose to side with the new Republic of Texas.

Scott ran for President of the new Republic of Texas and won. Soon after that he and Paula got married. They had two

children; Scotty and Pauline.

Although the war with the UN troops on the northern border was not over the fight was; for a while anyway.

Other Publications of

Vernon Gillen

Below is a list of my other novels and books that have been published.

Published Novels

1. "Texas Under Siege 1."

Tale of a Survival Group Leader.

After a man is voted as the leader of his survival group in Texas a self proclaimed Marxist president asked the United Nations troops to come in and settle down the civil unrest. The civil unrest was really nothing but Americans that complained about how he ran the country.

2. "Texas Under Siege 2."

The Coming Storms.

The young group leader continues to fight when the countries that made up the United Nations troops in the United States decided to take over parts of the country for their own country's to control.

3. "Texas Under Siege 3."

The Necro Mortises Virus.

As the group leader continues to fight the UN he learns that an old organization really controlled everything. They were known as the Bilderbergs. Tired of the resistance in Texas they release the Necro Mortises virus also known as the zombie virus.

4. "Texas Under Siege 4."

250 Years Later.

This novel jumps 250 years into the future where the

Bilderbergs are still living with modern technology while the other people have been reduced to living like the American Indians of the early 1800's. One of these young man stands up and fights the Bilderbergs with simples pears and arrows.

5. "The Mountain Ghost 1."

The Legend of Russell Blake.

After the Chinese and North Koreans attack the southern United States two young brothers, Brandon and Russell Blake go after the invading enemy. After Brandon is killed Russell smears a white past allover his exposed skin and earns the name Mountain Ghost.

6. The Mountain Ghost 2."

The Legend Continues.

The Mountain Ghost continues to fight the Chinese and North Koreans soldiers that have invaded the entire southern half of the United States.

7. "The Mountain Ghost 3."

The Ghost Soldiers.

After the death of Russell Black his son, Russ, continues as to bring death and destruction to the enemy as the new Mountain Ghost.

8. "The Mountain Ghost 4."

The Ghost Warriors.

After Russ and June have twin girls they grow up and move back south to fight the Chinese and North Koreans as the Ghost Twins. Before long they grow in numbers and call themselves the Ghost Warriors.

9. "Neanderthal 1."

As a child he was injected with alien DNA. While in the Navy he was injected with Neanderthal DNA. Now because of these two injection without his knowing young Michael

Gibbins changes into a six and a half foot tall Neanderthal from time to time. He grew up being bullied in school and wished that he could change into a monster so he could get back at them. Now he wishes he could take that wish back.

10. " Neanderthal 2."

Little Mary Ann, the daughter of Michael and Evie grows to the age of thirteen. As she grows she learns that he has many of the same abilities that her father had; and more. The problem is that she has a hard time controlling them and her anger. This causes problems for everyone watching over and trying to hide her.

11. "Neanderthal 3."

After Mary Ann grows up she sets out to find and rescue her father. After getting married she learns where her father is. She and her husband set out to rescue him. Will the family be a family again?

12. "My Alien Connections 1."

After learning that he has been abducted many times over the years sixty-four year old Bubba is asked to be a part in an alien experiment. He ends up falling in love with an alien hybrid that has known through all of his abductions.

But the Aliens, the Stylus are at war with another planet, the Zims. As their war continues the Zim try to take the twins born to Bubba and his alien hybrid wife who have been prophesied hundreds of years earlier. Do the Zim win or does Bubba win?

13. "My Alien Connection 2"

After the American President turns against Bubba he and Becka move to the planet Stylus. After a while the American President breaks his agreement with Yunnan, the leader of the Stylus world and Bubba goes on the attack. When the American President becomes an ally with the Zim home world the war

between Stylus and Zim thickens.

Through all of this Bubba and Becka must fight the Zim that are constantly trying to kidnap their twins which are the Prophecy Twins of Stylus. Fighting this war on many fronts Bubba is given control of Stylus warships and brings the fighting to the planet Zim.

14. "My Alien Connection 3"

As the Prophecy Twins grow up they learn many things and go through a few hardships. But they had always had each other until there is a betrayal in the family. Someone in the family turns to help the enemy causing problems for all Stylus.

How will Bubba and Becka handle this? How will the citizens of Stylus handle this? What will the twins do about this? Who even is the traitor?

15. Deadwalkers:

After terrorist drop three glass tubes from a skyscraper in New York City the Necro Mortisis Virus is released. Almost instantly zombies start multiplying and moving west. Within a few months they reach Texas and the Lawson family must fight the living as well as the dead to stay alive.

16. "The Glassy War 1."

Three thousand years in the future and three galaxies away the United Planet Counsel fight and enemy that is trying to control every galaxy they come to. After both star ships crash into the planet the survivors continue to fight.

17. The New Republic of Texas:

After the Republican President and Vic-President are assonated the Democrat Speaker of the House becomes the new President of the United States. Soon after that she becomes a Dictator.

American civilians pick up their rifles and fight back against this new communist dictatorship. But the hardest fighting is in

the state of Texas. Texas finally becomes free thanks to a young man named Scott Staninski. Standing tall and refusing to give in to the new American dictator he and others like him free the citizens of Texas and the new Republic of Texas is formed.

18. Seven Little Darlings:

Seven fallen angles, demons from Hell have a change of heart and try to return to Heaven. But God would not allow any fallen angles to return to heaven. When Satan learned about the seven fallen angles trying to return to Heaven he punished them by sending them into seven dolls. The fallen angles would now live out eternity imprisoned in these dolls.

For many years these seven dolls were considered collector's idems and found their way into an auction. A man bought the dolls for his five year old daughter. As the little girl grows she discovers that the dolls protect her. Death comes to anyone that hurts her. Her name is Jenifer but her father calls her Jen.

Other Published Books

1. "Carnivores of Modern Day Texas."

A study of the animals in Texas that will not only kill you but in most cases will eat you.

2. "Zombies; According to Bubba"

After studying the Necro Mortises virus for my novel *Texas Under Siege 3*, I realized that I had a great deal of information on it. After finishing the novel I wrote this book leaving the reader to make their own decision.

Unpublished

A great deal goes into publishing a novel or book that takes time. After I write a novel I have someone proofread it. Then I have to find an artist to draw the cover picture which is hard to do. Actually finding an artist is easy but finding one that I can

afford is not so easy. Then the novel or book has to be approved by the publishing company. Only then is it published. Then you have kindle and that opens another can of worms.

The fallowing novels are unpublished as I write this but will be published soon. Keep checking Amazom.com for any new novels that I have published.

1. "The Fire Dancers."

I stopped writing this novel to start writing the Mountain Ghost series but I will be getting back to it.

I hope that you have enjoyed this novel. Please help me by sending your comments on what you thought about this novel or book by contact me at bubbasbooks@msn.com . By doing this you will let me know what you, the public, are looking for in these types of novels and books. I have a very creative mind, a bit warped some say but, still creative. However; I still need to know what you are looking for. I thank you for your assistance in this.

Vernon Gillen

Made in the USA
Columbia, SC
16 November 2022